Flying Blind

ROSANNE HAWKE

For Paris and Tahlia, thank you for your
inspiration over the years.

Readers' comments on Flying Blind

What a lovely story you've written capturing the worries, confusion and heartache of a 15-year-old girl. I liked that the beach featured a lot and that tended to be her safe place. It was very easy to read. I like how she gradually gained insight into her friendships and learnt to understand herself more. You have been able to show what a real friend looks like.
Katie Hawke

A great read! I laughed, I related, and at times was on the edge needing to know what happens next! Another amazing story by Rosanne Hawke.
Helen Lamb

I just finished your book and oh my gosh I loved it. The horse-riding scene is sooo good, definitely my favourite.
It doesn't matter what people say about you. That's none of your business. Your job is to be yourself and shine, not worry about anyone else.
I really like this line, it's definitely something people my age should hear a whole lot more.
... that I can choose how to be treated. I write that Chloe doesn't belong in my head,
then I stop. Where does she belong? My pen scratches on the paper: in my heart.
That doesn't mean I have to agree with her opinions or put up with what she says,
just to want what's good for her.
I really like this too, it's a good way to put dealing with forgiveness in words.
Amelia Penner, 15 years.

Fliyng Blind

Published by Rhiza Edge, 2022
An imprint of Rhiza Press
P. O. Box 302
Chinchilla Qld 4413
Australia
www.wombatrhiza.com.au
© Rosanne Hawke, 2022

Cover and Layout by Rhiza Press

ISBN: 978-1-76111-039-9

A catalogue record for this
book is available from the
National Library of Australia

1

The waves pounce onto the shore just like the dogs do. Vinny gives a yip and splashes over them. Tyler follows him with a bark. I love this time of day, the sun's about to set, the wind's dropping. Soon the western sky will light up like illuminate art. That's when I see the birds—they look big enough to be pelicans—flying together in formation across the reddening sky. How do they know where they're going? I stand still, watching them, trying to imagine my worries washing off me, being flown out over the sea, gone forever. It doesn't work. Dad is still on my mind.

My very first memory of him was down here on the beach, an evening like this. I must have been two, though Mum wonders if I can remember that far back. I was toddling along the sand and fell face-first into one of those warm pools the tide leaves behind. My eyes stung and I couldn't move. Dad was there in a heartbeat, picking me up and holding me close while I screamed my outrage. Just like when I was born, he said. I don't remember those details, just him being there, so close, saving me. Growing up I never doubted his love. Never had to think about it; took it for granted.

Now I wonder: does he still love me? I hardly see him anymore, not since he accepted that managerial position at his work with all the overtime. He's good at maths, a talent I didn't inherit, but he used to help me do my homework. Now my marks are dropping. It's not just that. He never gets home in time for dinner, he never takes Merryn and me places like he used to. On weekends he's even at conferences down in Adelaide. We haven't been camping since forever. And I can't say anything about it to Mum. She's doing the best she can with work, home and us girls. It's a good opportunity for Dad, but I just wish he could spend more time with us. He's so tired at night he falls asleep on the couch, and I wish I could ask him a few things. Like about Ryan Kitto in Year 11. I was sitting with Chloe and Ashleigh (she's Ryan's sister) at lunch last week and Ryan walked past with a mate and grinned at me. What was that? Does he smile at everyone? Or does he like me? Chloe didn't seem to notice and that's another thing. She's my friend, well, it's like she decided I would be her friend when she came at the beginning of the year and she's been really nice, given me stuff, but there's something not consistent about the way she treats me lately and I can't put my finger on it. Just when I think I'll ask her about it she's nice again. Maybe I need to be a better friend to her.

Tyler puts a wet paw on my knee. He always knows when I'm obsessing. 'Do you want to play, boy?' He barks once and I chase him into the water.

The wispy dark bits in my mind blow away. I leave the boys in the shallows, drop my shorts and swim out further near the jetty. Here, I don't have to think about Dad or Chloe and Ashleigh who say I eat too much and should go to the gym. I'd rather swim.

It all fades away as I lay back and enjoy the rise and fall of the water beneath me. I roll over and breaststroke away from the shadow of the jetty. People have drowned in holes here. That's when I see the dark fin from the seaward side. I don't wait to get a second look—just fling myself into freestyle in the straightest line to the shore. Faster, Essie, faster. How quick can those things swim? Faster than you, Essie, a voice in my head snaps. This can't be the end, surely? I only just turned fifteen. So much more life to live. Just swim. That's all I have to do. Swim. I chant in my head like a cox on a rowboat. Faster. Faster. Faster.

I'm floundering by the time I reach the breaking waves. There's nothing behind me as far as I can see. No fins. Nor do I have the energy to swim into shore. Tyler and Vinny are barking as they watch out for me. I turn onto my back again before I sink. After a rest, I'll be fine to swim back to them. Sharks don't come in this close.

Then I feel it—a nudge. I collapse under the water. Just bump them on the nose, a fisherman on TV said once. Bump them back and they'll go. Stand your ground. I surface, spluttering, this time ready to fight. It's got hold of me round the middle. All those wildlife shows are right: it doesn't hurt at first. Then I hear the voice. 'Hey, it's okay. Easy.'

When I open my eyes, would you know it? Not a great white shark. But a great browned junior lifesaver. Ashleigh's older brother, Ryan Kitto, in the flesh. 'Looked like you were in trouble.'

It's difficult to talk with water still in my mouth. At least I tell myself that's the reason. He's good looking even when he's wet. And he's still got his arms around me. 'Thanks, but I'm okay.' I must have been making a hideous splash. 'I thought there was a shark.'

He scans the water behind me. No one is stupid enough to

ignore a shark warning. 'Nah,' he says finally. 'There were some dolphins out there before though.' Just my luck to miss seeing a dolphin up close because I was scared.

'It didn't jump.'

'Maybe you didn't wait long enough.' He's grinning. Pulling my leg? Who'd wait? Now I can tell he's teasing. His smile seems kind. The sun is setting as he glances at my mouth and leans closer like he's going to kiss me. But he stops a hand's width from my face, still smiling. 'You okay now?' Then he's checking the water around him—the lifesaver on duty—and I nod, releasing him of this one.

'See ya round then.' He lets go of me and throws himself into a wave. You couldn't say he *saved* me, not technically. It was more relief that he wasn't a shark, but the thought of what could have happened starts feeding the fantasies that can fill my head at times. Like, was he going to kiss me? It's hard to tell. There's that smile last week too. Ryan Kitto is hard not to notice. If a group of guys are playing sport on the oval, I can pick him out easy. It's just a dream, of course. But in most of the folk tale novels I read the guy is like Ryan, someone kind who stands out from the crowd. Imagine if someone like that cared about me, wanted to spend time with me and listened to my stories and concerns. I close my eyes. I can still feel where his hands were on my bare back. *Enough Essie, this is stupid.* I swim back to put a stop to Tyler's and Vinny's barking.

2

There's been a slight shift in the order of life at school this term when Jowan Tallack joins our class. Chloe says he's the most socially inept guy she's ever seen. Not as many muscles as Ryan—how can she tell, unless like me, she's seen Ryan's—and his hair is brown and past his ears, not short like Ryan's sundrenched locks. It's as if Jowan's a creature who Chloe doesn't need to waste breath on and yet, since he's come a spring breeze wafts into forgotten corners in our classroom, like dust lifting and settling when a door is opened and closed, and I can't remember how it started.

Maybe it began the first day of term. Ms Clemo was calling the roll, and everyone was mucking around as usual, except Jowan. He must have been listening for he actually called out 'here' when Ms Clemo said his name. We don't do that. Ms Clemo looks up each time she says our names to check we're there, we don't have to call out. People snickered. That was the second thing, he didn't turn red or blotchy like kids do when others laugh at them. It was like he didn't notice and just sneezed into a giant-sized tissue. He even says 'G'day' like country shows on TV. I mean, we're a long way from the city too but we don't say 'g'day'. There are losers in every class, Chloe says, but there's something interesting about Jowan that makes me think Chloe's wrong about him. He's just different. Unfortunately, I've discovered she takes it personally if you disagree with her, so I haven't disclosed my thoughts on Jowan Tallack.

Today I open my lunch dish on the Lunch Bench under the biggest pepper tree. This is another thing: I can't let Mum do my lunch anymore as she's likely to put in unhealthy stuff like highly processed cheese. My little sister Merryn loves plastic cheese, but it can't be good for her. I've bought a special dish with sections.

Chloe checks out my new lunch box. 'Hmm,' she says. 'Good on you, Essie, that's a good, healthy lunch.' It makes me warm inside, she can really make you feel appreciated. Ever since Chloe and Ashleigh have started going to the gym, they haven't eaten bread at school, only salad and fruit. Chloe and Ashleigh never go to the canteen since they think it doesn't have healthy food. I can see their point, but if we want the canteen to stock an item like salad in a bowl, we could always ask for it.

Brett, the trainer at the gym, gave Ashleigh this special diet to follow. Chloe reckons that's why Mary's big: she likes pies. But here's the thing, Mary's not big at all. She's just not as skinny as Chloe, and who is? Certainly not me. Mary and I used to sit in the lunch shed at primary school in our town, sauce from a pasty dribbling down our chins. I still like them, though I've not said so. I'd like to sit with Mary again eating a Ned Kelly pie, egg and bacon set into it, and let myself savour the taste. But I'd never hear the end of it from Chloe. She says pies are so unhealthy and all Australia's diseases can be traced back to the sausage. Ashleigh says Brett and Ryan think girls who eat pastry and sausages are such a turn-off.

Today, Mary pulls out a Cornish pasty with extra pastry

crimped on top (her mother bakes them) and Laila starts on her curry in a wrap. Chloe stares at them pointedly while she snaps carrot sticks with her teeth. But Mary and Laila don't seem to care.

Ashleigh says, 'What are you doing this weekend, Laila?'

Laila shrugs. 'Family stuff.' Her family came from Iran a few years ago and they're often having dinners with their community.

Chloe doesn't join in the conversation, but Ashleigh asks Mary the same question.

'Tennis,' Mary says.

'Tennis?' Chloe's head shoots up.

'Yeah, and footy in the winter. The school's got a girls' team this year.'

Chloe's eyes grow wide. I can't tell what she's thinking. Surely sport must be good, right? Talking about sport, I hope that Ashleigh will invite me over one weekend, then I'd get to see Ryan. Ashleigh doesn't get to ask me what I'll be doing this weekend, as Chloe launches into her weekend plans.

'I'm getting my hair coloured.' She stares deliberately at Mary's brown bob and Laila's hijab scarf. Bet she's thinking there's no point getting your hair coloured if you're going to cover it up. She glances at my hair. 'You know, Essie, yours could be blond like mine and Ashleigh's if you had it coloured. Guys like Ryan prefer blond hair.' I stare at her. Only last week she said my hair was a pretty honey brown.

'And you could wear coloured contacts so your eyes aren't so green. The guys I know like blue.' That would include Ryan too, I guess.

Am I frowning? I try not to show her words hurt. So, she has blue eyes but I can't believe what I'm hearing today. I've got a prickling behind my nose but I don't want to make a scene. Chloe steals a glance at me and I smile to show it doesn't matter. But it's not true.

Mary sighs. 'Who cares what guys like?'

'You should.' Chloe says this like Mary in particular needs to take notice. She's about to say more when the siren goes for sports practice. Mary packs her lunch away and gives me a grin as she leaves. Laila joins her.

I appreciate Mary's honesty, but Chloe might be on to something. Would it be worth making changes so a guy like Ryan would notice me more? There's no point thinking about it as Dad wouldn't let me colour my hair anyway. He'd say, that is, he *used* to say, that I look fine without makeup. When I'd moan about having a cold sore he'd squint at my face and say, 'Where?' Then he'd kiss me as close as possible to where it was. I miss that. I'm quiet as I finish my lunch; Chloe's comments about my hair and eyes have dried up my words. Ashleigh is going on about how Brett kisses. There are a few other things Ashleigh sighs about too and even stuff she only tells Chloe in whispers.

No point in me saying anything, even if I felt like it, as Chloe ignores me if I don't add to the conversation she's started. It's taboo to start a new one. I've tried. Besides, what can I say? Chloe and Ashleigh would be horrified if they knew I hadn't been kissed by a guy. Nearly though, or was that just my fancy? Imagine the expressions on their faces. Incredulous. They might decide I'm too inexperienced to be recommended to Ryan for a date. I've never had a boyfriend except for the silly note changing that went on in Year 6 and judging by the way Ryan treated me at the beach he would be a caring guy to go out with.

Jowan Tallack's at the bus stop this afternoon when I walk past with Chloe and Ashleigh. Since it's Thursday, Chloe's brother is giving Chloe and me a ride back to our town. The high school is in the biggest inland town on the peninsula and kids bus in from all over. Ashleigh says, 'Poor Chloe. It's weird that a girl like you has a brother who is such a geek.' Chloe's embarrassed about it and tells him to park down the end of the street so no one has to walk past his car, a true rusted rattler. When Brett of the Circuit comes to pick up Ashleigh, she stands in the Year 12 car park, so he'll think she's nearly eighteen and makes sure everyone notices him in his Corvette. He always drives it with the soft cover down.

'Essie.' I turn. It's Jowan.

'Hey.'

He's standing next to Josephine Reynolds. Josephine is Chloe's idol. She's returned to do Year 12 as a mature student. I was surprised to discover Chloe had a person she looked up to. She seems to know so much. Josephine is the Magor house sports captain, looks like a beach model even in school uniform, and can do no wrong according to Chloe. I glance at her now. It's not just that she has a figure like a model, she has grace. When she walks it's a fluid movement, like water gently flowing over rocks in a dry creek bed, and even though there's no sound, people stop at the wonder of it. Josephine doesn't even seem to notice the ripples she causes.

Whatever Jowan was going to say I don't get to hear as Chloe's spotted Erik parked closer than usual to the main gate.

'In the car, quick,' she says with a glance over her shoulder that could win her a role in *Mission Impossible*. Only Ashleigh seems to understand Chloe's horror. I see her sympathetic smile before we turn the corner. That's when I see Ryan walk up beside her and lift his hand in a half-wave. It can't be, but it seems like he's looking at me.

Erik apologises. 'Sorry, weren't any other parks today.'

I can't see what's wrong with Erik. He's cute and cuddly like a bear, but Chloe sighs and says that his weight shows a disregard for social norms and his fashion sense is stuck in a time warp. Chloe can't be seen with him as it will totally destroy the image she's working hard to build up. This is where I should be wondering if I need to be hearing all this stuff and start sticking up for the people Chloe bags—when I remember Ryan's smile after he fished me out of the sea. That expression in his eyes when he leaned closer. Maybe I can put up with what Chloe says just to see him look at me like that again. Besides, Chloe can be really nice when she's in a good mood.

Erik and Chloe drop me off at my corner and the dogs are already scratching at the gate. It's nice to be greeted ecstatically, even if they are dogs. I hug them both around the neck, Tyler first then Vinny, and narrowly escape getting my face eaten. 'Okay, boys. Later, I'll take you for a run on the beach.' They sit back, their tongues lolling. If I'm lucky I'll see Ryan training near the Life Saving Club.

Mum's not home from picking up Merryn from the local primary school, so I grab a juice and get some TV in before piano practice. It's a show called *Love Online*. I'd rather see what I'm getting. Like Ryan. I wonder if he thinks of me.

My mind wanders to the comment Chloe made today about my eyes. The first week of school she gravitated towards me and paid me lots of compliments. She'd met Ashleigh before school started as their families already knew each other before Chloe's moved into the marina, and so I was surprised Chloe was so taken with me, quite frankly. I'm not what she'd call popular, like Ashleigh.

'Hey,' Chloe said to me the first day. 'What lovely green eyes you have.' She made me feel like Red Riding Hood's wolf.

What a strange thing to say when first meeting someone. I didn't know whether to thank her or what, so I just grinned like an ass. So, it was baffling today when she suggested coloured contacts would help me. Did I misunderstand her the first time? Or is she forgetful?

3

This evening Merryn and I make dinner together. I haven't spent as much time with her this year as I usually do. There's more homework in Year 10 and Chloe has wanted me to visit when I'd normally be with Merryn. Mum's concerned because she hasn't met Chloe's mum yet. Nor have I, but I haven't let on.

'Can we make lasagne?' Merryn says.

'Sure.' But we don't have pasta sheets. I Google on my phone. 'Hey,' I say. 'We have eggplant. Let's make eggplant lasagne. It'll be healthy and probably taste the same.' I look in the fridge. 'Here's ricotta.' I get it out and the parmesan cheese. 'Garlic, tins of tomatoes in the pantry. We have everything.' I smile at Merryn.

She looks unsure. 'Eggplant?'

'You'll love it.' I put her to work cutting the eggplant and salting it. She screws up her face. 'Don't worry, we'll wipe the salt off in a minute.'

I'm chopping onions when she hits me with this: 'Why don't you go on a date with Jowan Tallack?'

'What?' I stare at her, shocked. Then I say the first excuse that pops in my head. 'I'm in Year 10 and so is Jowan. He's not old enough to drive so how can he take me on a date?' More importantly, I don't know him.

'You could walk along the beach. Get a milkshake at the Beach Café. Like you used to do with me.'

I frown at her, trying to ignore the comment about her and me. 'How do you know Jowan?'

She shrugs. 'Saw him on the beach when I went down with Mum. He's got a nice sister. We're friends already.' This brings a smile to her face. 'Rebecca.'

'Hmm.' I turn back to cook the bolognaise.

Dinner is a success, except Dad doesn't manage to get home in time. Mum says to start anyway. She doesn't like our digestive systems mucked about by having dinner too late. She puts Dad's on a plate for him to heat up later in the microwave. Merryn and I share a look. This is one thing we're agreed on: Dad needs to be home more. Mum always says it's important to eat together around the table. But what's the point when Dad doesn't bother?

After tea, Dad's still not home. Merryn goes to Maypole Dancing with Mum, who helps teach it as she used to do it when she was young. Every second year we have the Kernewek Lowender, the world's largest Cornish festival on the peninsula. That's when the Maypole dancing happens. When I was in primary school I loved the thrill of the wind in my hair as we danced and watched the ribbons make patterns around the pole as we wove them up and over each other. So much fun.

Before I get the boys' leads for a walk, I dash off a note for Dad: *I'm down at the beach. Essie.* I draw a love heart. Maybe he'll come to find me.

The dogs are excited as usual. 'C'mon, boys.' I undo their leads and they race off. We run some, then stop near the jetty. I watch them enjoy themselves, jumping and trying to catch the waves. Vinny looks almost feline, grinning as he pounces on the foam. Tyler rushes further in, his back undulating like a hairy dolphin jumping hurdles, yelping and flapping his tail in joy. The beach is golden retriever heaven and the boys aren't shy in expressing their worship. I wish I could be like them. I glance behind me at the Life Saving Club. Ryan could be looking out that window right now or maybe he's jogging up the beach.

The water is up to my knees and I get splashed by Vinny skimming a wave. At times like this, I wish I was still ten like Merryn. Life is so simple at ten. I don't remember ever thinking about what to wear, how to do my hair, where I had to be and how and when, and with whom. When I was ten, I was like Tyler and Vinny, enjoying the world, getting told off sometimes by Mum and Dad, but I had a running-free type of life when I look back on it. At ten I believed. At ten I had joy.

Maybe hindsight is always rosy? It just seems that there are so many rules at my age, so much to be careful of. Just to be seen frolicking with dogs may not be Ryan's idea of cool for all I know. Hanging around with Ashleigh and Chloe will help me get to know him better at least. They seem to understand all the right things to do. They should put out a guide about it: *Dummy's Survival Guide for Fifteens.* They'd make millions.

After all my hoping for a glimpse of Ryan, it's Jowan who strides onto the beach, preceded by a gang of little kids already in swimmers and wound up to excitement pitch. They pounce almost as high as Vinny and screech as they run into the water. They're a mass of brown ponytails, water wings and excited shouts. See what I mean about being a little kid? They just enjoy the moment and don't obsess.

'G'day.' That's Jowan. For a moment he reminds me of

Crocodile Dundee.

'Hi. They all yours?' I hope I don't sound horrified.

'Yeah. And a ring-in from next door.' He doesn't even look embarrassed about having to watch his siblings in the water. Mum doesn't let me do that with Merryn.

'So where are you from?' I could kick myself for being unimaginative.

Turns out the Tallacks have moved here from further north, the Outback basically. 'Dad's a grazier,' Jowan says. 'though we had cattle, but it wasn't going so well. Drought, you know. There was even a fire near us, too close. Besides, there's my hay fever and Luke has asthma. They thought the sea would be better at the moment. Give us a breather.'

I'm shocked about the bushfire. 'The fire must have been scary.'

'Yeah.' That's all he says and I don't like to probe.

We're quiet, listening to the wash of the water as it pulls back, the kids' squeals and Tyler and Vinny's excitement at having playmates, while I try to imagine Dad giving up his life's dream so I'd feel better. The image doesn't materialise. *Up north.* No wonder the kids are enthralled with the beach.

'Do you find school okay?' I've never had a chance to even talk to him at school. He always seems happy enough in class.

'Sure. Much bigger than our school. We only had one small class for each year level, not three like here. The work's much the same, I guess.'

I don't want to talk too much about school, even though I started it—I like my weekends off. 'What will your dad do here?'

'Try to sell cars, or farmhand work. For a while anyway. Mum's a teacher and all the kids are at school now.' He points them out. 'Luke, Desi, Rebecca. Tad's started kindy. So, she'll go back relieving.'

15

Selling cars sounds boring to me after living on the land but I don't say anything out of respect for his feelings. If I told Chloe that Jowan came from the Outback, she'd say it figured: no wonder he knows nothing and doesn't fit in. But I doubt Jowan would wear that.

He asks about me then. 'You always lived here?' It takes me by surprise.

'Yeah.' There isn't much to say. Dad's great-great-grandfather used to work on the wharf at Port Adelaide after he came from Cornwall. Then he came up here when the Moonta mines opened. He had land here before it spread into housing estates. 'Our family has been here since the 1860s,' I say.

The sun's spreading salmon pink streaks in the sky as if it's blotting paper seeping into the sea. Jowan gets philosophical about it and starts talking about the lost land of Lyonnesse. How the sea there must have been this beautiful. If he talks like this to guys at school, he'll have no show of making friends. Yet it doesn't seem so strange to me, standing here watching a sunset and thinking about what could have been. And what might be.

Jowan surprises me with this quip. 'I wonder if it was a night like this Sir Lancelot began his quest for the Holy Grail.'

When I was a kid, I liked those Arthur stories. Apparently, Jowan still does.

'I have this book,' he says, 'that proves where Avalon is.'

'It's in Cornwall,' I say, remembering what Dad said about it. 'Sunk under the sea on the way out to the Scilly Isles.' He grins at me as if he's impressed I know anything about it at all.

'It's in Wales,' he says then.

'With a name like Tallack, I thought you'd be patriotic at least.' Everyone in Britain claims King Arthur as their own. Even Scotland lays claim to him at some point in time, but Dad said that was stretching the imagination a bit far.

'Have to face facts sometime,' Jowan says, monitoring his gang of siblings with half-shut eyes. Tyler and Vinny have just worked out how much fun it is being splashed by little kids. They're returning the favour. Vinny looks like a bucking horse on a merry-go-round and Rebecca and her friend squeal as the spray covers them from sight. 'In the old days they just got the names on the maps wrong. They thought Kernyw meant Cornwall, as in Kernow? But it was a place in Wales.'

'Really?' I let my tone show how unconvinced I am, but Jowan doesn't bite. Instead, he invites me back to his house. To see his evidence no doubt. Bet he's a fantasy geek and grew up on Tolkien. I decline. Graciously, I hope. But Merryn's talk of dating him looms in my mind. What if I was walking off the beach with Jowan and his mob, and Ryan emerged from the Life Saving Club? He'd think I already had a boyfriend and that would be the end of that.

When I come in after putting the dogs around the back, Dad's in the lounge. 'I'm sorry Es. I had to finish a report.' I can't see the note on the table. Has he kept it? I try not to act disappointed, but I feel like huffing.

'I'll make us a hot chocolate,' I say instead, 'and we can chat.'

He smiles but I can tell he's tired. He looks so much older, slumped there on the couch. Mum and Merryn won't be home for a bit yet. I bring the mugs into the lounge and what do you know. Dad's fallen asleep. In front of the footy show too. I turn the TV down and carefully lay a rug over him. I put his mug in Merryn's room and sip mine in bed, reading a novel retelling the folktale of the swan brothers.

4

Sunday, and Mum's not on shift at the nursing home today so we go to church together. It's the highlight of my week—not. I shouldn't be so cynical as at least I get to see Dad. He reckons Christianity has pulled generations of our family through thick and thin ever since they came from Cornwall. Generations of miners, wharfies and farmers, he says when he gets going. Now he's an executive in a company but I'm a bit hazy on what he actually does. Dad's the only one in his family who's kept up the church going. Uncle Greg said he saw the light and stopped believing all that rubbish years ago. Dad always winces when he says that, but I bet Uncle Greg says it on purpose.

Mum loves everybody, though it gets spread a little thin at times. She puts her energy into her nursing, Merryn, Dad, the dogs, and me. Did I mean to say it in that order? When I was five, before Merryn was born, I'd wonder why they only had one kid. Maybe I was adopted? What sort of a kid thinks that? Nothing wrong with being adopted, unless you're not told. *What secret are they hiding?* I'd wonder. I'd have this dream of getting lost at the beach and calling for Mum, and all these women would drift past one by one and none had her face. No one wanted me. One night I woke up crying and Mum rushed in. It's then in the middle of the night that you say what you dream and fear, not in the morning when you know it was silly. Mum was horrified. 'Whatever made you think you were adopted?' I couldn't remember. What is it that makes kids believe stuff? Some conversation that they hear the tail-end of, a movie? Or something the parent does that seems to prove it? And one day it all adds up, like a sum you get the answer to but don't have the workings-out for. Mum cut some of her shifts after that.

Today Dad doesn't like the length of my skirt, or should I say the shortness thereof, but at least I have his attention. This skirt is not as short as Chloe's. I have to be careful, best not to have things exactly like Chloe's and Ashleigh's. Just enough to obtain the same look. They think being a try-hard is worse than not fitting in at all.

Mrs Dunleavy greets us at the door. She has a smile like a tiger. I often wonder why they let her be a welcomer. She'd scare an outlaw biker away. Another thing that would scare anyone coming in off the street is the ancient music, the nice dresses of the olds, and mostly the lack of teenagers. No one from school goes here, which mightn't be a bad thing. Dad likes it because it's small and it's the same denomination his ancestors belonged to. But hello? I'm not an ancestor. I'd like to know what's going on, to be able to enjoy it at least, if that's possible. They still use the original King James Bible. There are so many *thous* and *knowests* you can't get the drift of the story. Need I say more?

The other good thing about church is seeing Nanna and Grandad. This was the actual church Dad grew up in. His parents sit in the pew in front of us so they can hear better since there's a loop for those who have hearing devices. All their friends still come, except the ones in aged care. Merryn sometimes sits with

Nanna, but I don't always do that. Nanna understands those sorts of things. Besides, today I want to sit with Dad.

'How's your piano going?' Nanna turns slightly to smile at me.

'Good.' I lean forward so she can hear. 'I'd like to play some modern music but my lessons are all classical.' I'm also predicting what Chloe would say if she found out I play classical.

Nanna's eyes twinkle at me. 'Have you asked your teacher about that?'

I shake my head and smile at her as the organ starts playing. She looks so cute today—she's wearing leggings and an upbeat long top.

During the opening prayer, I check out my fingernails. Might let them grow like Laila's. She and her mother always have creative nails. It'll stuff up my piano playing, but Chloe's quite firm that classical music is not cool. Nanny's right, maybe I should ask, but what would Mrs Mangledorf say?

Here comes the first chorus, nothing like Handel's 'Hallelujah Chorus' even though that word features strongly in this one too. Last week Dad said happily, 'It's so nice singing songs I remember from my childhood.' He doesn't even realise he's left me with a ritual of relics. Today he seems preoccupied. He used to hold my hand during prayers and grin at me when we sang.

Then I hear a sneeze. I know that sound from school— allergic, hay-fevery—it couldn't be.

During the next prayer, I check. Yep. Jowan Tallack. Almost the whole left side of the church is filled with his family. What do I do now? I don't always listen to the sermon so this time I think I'll devote the time to deciding what to do about Jowan. Do I order him on pain of death not to let on he saw me here in case Chloe, and therefore Ashleigh, and therefore Ryan, find out? Mary and Laila know I go to church but judging by some things Chloe's said lately she wouldn't think it was cool. I groan inside. Why should it matter? When I spent time with Mary and Laila last year everything was fine. It's a pity Chloe doesn't like me spending time with other girls. Commitment in bestie friendships is everything, she says.

The sermon starts. It's about ten bridesmaids. When I hear the word 'bridesmaid' I almost pull up my head in interest, but I stop myself in time. I listen with my head down. I hear about these ten girls—imagine having ten bridesmaids!—waiting with oil in their lamps for the bridegroom to appear. The organised five buy more oil when he's later than usual. Apparently, weddings can be late in the Middle East. Aunty Joy went to a Pakistani one in Adelaide, and the bride was three hours late. The guests got fed well though.

Five bridesmaids in the story don't bother to keep watch and fall asleep. They must have left their lamps on, for when the bridegroom finally comes their oil has run out and they have to run to get more. When they return, they're too late and miss out on the party.

It's a message about being prepared for the second coming, we're told. But I can't stop thinking about those girls with no oil. Were they younger? Maybe only fifteen? How awful to miss out on everything. It sounds like me, flying in the dark and so unprepared for life.

It shocks me to realise I've listened to a whole sermon and I'm still sitting in the pew so stunned that Jowan comes up to me before I've decided what to say to him.

'Nice to see you, Essie.' There's a definite pressure on the word 'you'. He looks good today in long cream cargo pants, like Ryan wears. He's wearing boots and holding an Akubra hat in his left hand. I pull my thoughts into line and try to keep cool.

'Yeah,' is all I say and his smile fades slightly. I can't have him getting ideas, like Merryn. Just because we're the only two young people in church does not mean we're meant for each other. That would be divine intervention and it wouldn't be fair. Doesn't God give you the desires of your heart? My heart and what's in it must be painfully transparent in heaven.

Jowan follows me out to the lawn while the olds chew the fat over cups of tea and biscuits. 'So why did your family pick the peninsula to move to?' I say.

'Mum grew up here, so it's no big deal for her to come back. Good thing she came north though. Dad mightn't have married otherwise.' I must be staring—what an incredible thing to tell a person you've just met—because he adds defensively, 'It's real hard to meet girls when you're a farmer up north. Dad only met Mum because she was up there teaching. She's a music teacher, but she had a go at everything.'

I almost ask why his dad didn't try 'Farmer Wants a Wife'. Instead, I say, 'How come the interest in all things Celtic?'

'All Dad's people were Cornish—miners and farmers—'

I nod. 'Like us.'

He grins. It's not so weird. With the amount of migration from the UK that happened here in the nineteenth century, there's a 20 per cent chance (more on the peninsula, Dad says) of meeting a person with a Cornish background. Just as I thought, Jowan's mother introduced him to Tolkien when he was a kid and he's loved fantasy ever since.

'Arthur fascinates me,' he says, 'how people needed to hang on to a story like that.'

'To believe he was coming back?'

'Yep. Their lives must have been hard. Living under the Normans.'

I can't believe I'm discussing King Arthur again and I'm actually interested. We're staring out through the pines at the sea. You can see parts of it from here, the horizon blending in with the sky like two different shades of feathers under a duck's wing.

Just then, two of Jowan's brothers rush out, the screen door banging wide open, letting the flies buzz inside to the welcome coolness. Don't boys have any other speed? Merryn will be in there sipping cordial with her friend Madeline and Rebecca probably, comparing how many nibbles it takes to reach the toes of their teddy-bear biscuits.

'Jowan!' shouts Desi. Luke lags behind. I find out later they're twins. 'You have to come meet the minister.' I have a vision of Vinny as Desi jumps to a halt by Jowan and eyes me off. All he needs is fur and a tail and I'd know what to do with him. Jowan gives me a wish-I-could-stay grin and follows his brothers in. I've counted about five of them all together. They'd need a bus with that many kids. Bet Reverend Oldfield is happy they've come. He's doubled his junior congregation in one dollop.

It's then I realise I haven't dealt with my problem. How not to have Chloe or Ryan know that I come here? A curl of guilt catches in my gut. Why should it matter if they know? I didn't care who knew when I was ten and I believed all the stories. Jowan seems a friendly guy, but with no sense of what matters, he might tell. Who does he know that Chloe knows? As far as I can tell she doesn't have many friends yet and no one's likely to ask him in the middle of a game of cricket, 'Oh and by the way, does Essie Pederick go to church?' Course not. People say there's no discrimination here, what you believe is your private business. Ha! Who am I trying to kid? Nobody on TV goes to church except in ancient shows like *The Little House on the Prairie* or *Seventh Heaven*. Imagine characters in *Home and Away* praying about their problems. And I can just hear Ryan's tone if he found out. 'You go to church, that's, um, cool.' He'd nod his head a little and wouldn't smile. But his emphasis on cool would mean it wasn't at all. Being a Christian may be a free ticket to eternity, but in Chloe's eyes, and probably Ryan's, it's a direct flight to Loser-dom.

After stir-fry lunch, Dad finishes some work on his laptop. Wish I could talk to him about Chloe and Ryan. Right from the beginning of the year, since Chloe's taken an interest in me, I've spent a lot of time with her and Ashleigh. It was really good at first and it still is most of the time, but every now and then Chloe goes for me and I don't know why. It's so confusing. She's caught on that I like Ryan. Did I say that he 'rescued' me from the beach? Of course not. Maybe he told Ashleigh. What would I say to Dad? That I like a boy in Year 11 and I don't know if he likes me? Dad would say I don't need a boyfriend. What about Chloe? Why does she bother me? I want to be friends but at times she's not all that friendly, even though she was at the beginning of term. Then, she even gushed over me and gave me one of her tops, but she doesn't do that much now. And I don't know what I've done wrong.

I send Dad a text: *Hey, let's catch up on the jetty one afternoon this week. Love you.*

Right at the end of the jetty where you can't see any land is our favourite place. I can't remember how it started. Just that Dad would buy ice-creams and we'd walk all the way to the end and sit there, our legs hanging through the rails while I pretended we were floating on the water. Once we saw a sealion pup hanging around the pylons. That day we waited until it finally swam out to sea.

5

It's Monday after school and I'm trying to do my piano practice in our open space kitchen-dining area. Mum wants me to do more music exams, but I'm sick of them. I love piano but I'm still not sure about the music Mrs Mangledorf gives me. She is so ancient she must have given King David his harp lessons. She thinks everyone is learning piano to be a world-famous concert pianist, but I'm not. Nor have I plucked up the courage yet to tell her as Nanna suggested.

I start on the new Beethoven piece she's given me. The left hand has to play a different rhythm from the right. It's not so easy, nor is it working. Why can't everything be as easy as 'Für Elise'? I pull out some sheet music from the piano stool. I'll try something else to warm up.

My hands are straying over the piano keys now and suddenly I'm whisked away to the 'Middle of the Night'. The clack of my fingernails keeps up a rhythm as well, nice. Mum comes in at the coda.

'That's lovely, Eseld.' It's her lead-in phrase and I know what's coming next. 'Doesn't sound like one of your usual pieces?'

'No. I think I might play some more popular music. Can

we buy some online?'

'We'll see.' When Mum seems vague, it's exactly as it sounds: she doesn't want to think about it right now. Tired from lifting oldies onto bedpans all day. She still manages to notice the nails though. 'Eseld, how can you play the piano with those?' It's not a question: it's my first warning. I think I'll move my piano to my room.

Mum chops vegies on the bench and my nails clack some more on the keyboard when my phone vibrates. I pull it out of my pocket. It's Chloe. She hardly ever rings me anymore. What can she want? I get a quiver in my middle as I answer and it's not excitement.

'Hey, Chloe.' I try to sound upbeat, not as wary as a bird caught in a cat enclosure.

'Essie—thought we could watch some movies at my house after gym Friday night. Okay?'

My mouth opens and closes again. I think I'm in shock. It's been weeks since she's invited me to her house.

'Essie? Are you there?'

'Sure, thanks, see you Friday night.' I'm wondering if Ashleigh would be there and if so, will Ryan drop her off. Mum's trying not to let on she's listening, but she's as subtle as the huge knife she's chopping the onions with. I should have gone to my room. Chloe ends the call almost immediately. That was pretty business-like. No 'How are you?' or 'Watcha doing?'

'Um, Eseld ... do you think spending a lot of time with Chloe is a good idea?'

Here it comes. 'Why not?'

Mum trots out her standard parental concerns: 'We don't know them well, do we? Her family is so well off—um—will her mother be home this time? And who else will be there? There

26

might be alcohol—' She's not explaining it well and I don't feel like making it easy for her. I'm a bit nervous myself, but I can't tell Mum that, can I? She might suggest I shouldn't go.

'We're only going to watch movies.' This alarms her even more.

'What sort of movies?'

'She didn't say. Just movies.' I open up my Secret Garden music book, I love their Celtic sound. 'There's no need to worry, Mum.'

But for once she's right.

Chloe's house faces onto the marina. Dad said it used to be a swamp when he was a kid and one day all those fancy homes might sink into a bog. Mum told him off for having 'sour grapes', which started Merryn asking for some and getting upset when he didn't have any grapes at all. Chloe even has a private jetty running out over the water. When I first visited her, it was a blur of cream thick carpet, Italian tiles and gold tap wear in the bathroom. Change that to plural. On subsequent visits, I have counted no less than five loos and that may not be the extent of it. Anyway, that was the sum of what I could remember when Mum asked. She also caught on there were no adults in sight. I have still not met Chloe's olds. Even Erik's been out each time I've visited.

'Hey.' Chloe meets me at the door and takes me to the lounge. I hope she notices I'm wearing the top she gave me. It's a shiny pastel blue. She looks me up and down. 'You could have worn a top that's age-appropriate. You look like a baby.' Doesn't she remember she gave it to me? She acted like she was giving me something special. There's a prickling behind my eyes. Any confidence I had when I arrived has vanished. It's like she knows. 'Don't be so sensitive, Essie.'

Ashleigh walks in with a platter. 'Ryan's coming back later,' she says to Chloe. My heart gives a skip and I try to forget what Chloe said. Another girl from school, Lisa, turns up and brings her boyfriend. He looks like a junk-mail model. He giggles too much though, and it's a bit off-putting. I try not to stare. His friend, Derek, walks in. He has the booze. Dad would flip his lid. Wouldn't you know it? Neither Chloe nor Ashleigh organise booze. It comes from a friend of a friend. Just like Mum says. I wish she wasn't right about so many things. Derek with the six-packs doesn't remotely look eighteen. Guess some bottle shops don't have time to check ID, or he has an older brother.

Chloe gives Derek a grin and I can see why he's invited. She's busy putting nibbles into bowls: carrot sticks, celery, hummus. Derek's standing close by, helping where no help is needed, both of them grinning at nothing, their hands in each other's way. That leaves me the only one in the room without a boyfriend.

The first Netflix movie is the usual feel-good M-rated romp. Lots of unzipping, bare skin and the best girl gets the gorgeous bloke after a lot of conversations being misunderstood. Mum acts as if half the Hollywood movies are spawned in hell but she's a worrywart. It doesn't affect us. See? Lisa and her boyfriend are kissing on the couch—they're not even watching. The story's not bad, the rotten guy loses, falls off a cliff actually. So good wins over evil.

Derek's passing around bottles. Then he opens his laptop and streams to the TV. Looks like the next movie is on his computer. 'We're sweet,' he says. 'Good thing I have a VPN.' Lisa and the boyfriend keep kissing through the ads and when the movie starts, I can tell it's not my scene. If I was at home, channel hopping, I'd switch to the next one quick, but I can't do anything here. The beginning scene is one of those dark alleys, the camera hand-held to give you the impression you're right there. The music builds, there's a girl walking ahead, not glancing behind. The camera stalks her. I feel ill and I just know from the music it's going to be a rape. Maybe Lisa's boyfriend knows too; he's watching now, Lisa's sipping beer.

Something's wrong. The girl's not screaming and she should be. Maybe it's a comedy. I glance across at Ashleigh. I thought she'd have more style but she's grinning and the guys are laughing. Why don't I walk out?

Just then Ryan strides in and gets handed a beer. He frowns at first, then he sits, glued, giving a chuckle every now and then, but they aren't the kind you give at sitcoms. There's a dark shadow in the room, not helped by the smoke from Derek's vape and the sickly smell that's wafting over from his way. It's as if we're in the future where the atmosphere in a movie can infiltrate your room, and suddenly I realise what the movie is: soft porn. I've never seen one before and this is one too many. Just once I wish Mum had forbidden me to come. Forget I said that. I wish I could walk out, but I sit here, trying not to watch. It's the longest hour and twenty minutes of my life. My mind will be scarred.

'Drink, Essie?'

I'm about to shake my head at Chloe when I catch Ryan looking over at me. Sizing me up? Remembering who I am? Or is that a reflective look? I hold out my glass.

'Just half,' I say, trying to sound as though I've had enough and I'm mature enough to know.

Chloe snorts. 'Don't be a wimp all your life, Essie,' and she fills it up. I give a weak grin and hope Ryan didn't hear that. If it weren't for him I'd go. I've had enough. Lisa and her boyfriend have disappeared, and the beer has such a bitter taste.

Chloe smirks at me. 'You'll get used to it.' She likes red wine. She said since we live in the best wine-making state in the country we should get used to it young. I can just imagine Dad letting me do that. Not likely.

Then Ryan comes to perch on my side of the couch. I try not to think it may have to do with the fact that we are the only singles here. Except for Ashleigh. She couldn't very well bring Brett or he may catch on to how young she is.

'Good to see you. Essie, isn't it?' I nod, breathless as well as speechless. Is he remembering that fake shark attack? Yep.

'Seen any more sharks lately?' He's grinning, making conversation. I'm glad Mum can't see him now or she would say *he* was the shark. Sitting through that movie with his eyes red from drinking beer doesn't show him to his full advantage. But I stayed through the movie too. Maybe he just didn't know how to walk out either. He sits on the couch beside me so that our hips touch and he holds my hand. No guy has ever held my hand. I forget the beers he must have drunk and enjoy the warmth of my hand enclosed in his. He strokes my thumb and it tingles. Then he stops. I look across at him and I can see he's almost asleep. I leave my hand in his, a tiny hope rising in me like a baby bird's wing.

In the night I dream of Dad. I'm flying way above the clouds. It should be amazing but dark birds are tracking me, gaining on me. I look towards the sun and it blinds me. I keep flying. If I go fast enough, I'll keep in front. But I can hear their wings rustling, drawing closer. Louder. They must be huge. I'll be dinner for sure. Then another bird darts in from the left. It's Dad. He presses his face next to mine. It's like he's holding me up on the wind. I can see again and we're flying faster. Then suddenly he falls back, and I spin—round and round, lower and lower, faster and faster. The dark birds dive after me. I see their huge beaks open wide. So close.

I wake, breathless. It takes a moment in the dark to remember I'm not a bird. I wish I could crawl into Mum's and Dad's bed like when I was small. I can't tell Dad about the movie night, but I want to feel his arms around me, making me feel treasured. To remind me who I am.

6

A new customer walks into the gift shop and I try to smile. I'm still tired from the weekend and my sleepless nights since. A few days a week after school, and on Saturday mornings, I work in Aunty Joy's gift shop. It's called 'Gifts of Joy'. She loves fossicking out little things that people call treasures but can never find for themselves. Some customers are regulars and don't even go down to the city to shop for gifts. What's not here, Aunty Joy will find for them. Anything at all from classy glassy to gimmicky, weddings to Father's Day. She gift-wraps for free too. I've just finished a customer spiel on all the latest candles. I must have been persuasive because now there are so many to wrap.

At each fold of the paper, I can't stop thinking about Ryan saying 'Hi' to me outside the school gate this morning. Considering I'm only in Year 10, it's a bit of a social risk for him so maybe he does like me a little. I could tell he wanted to chat but a mate of his rushed up and whisked him away. And then when I got to my locker I find a note had been slipped in underneath. A corner was still poking out. When I opened the door, I found the note was from Ryan. I've read it so many times, I know it off by heart: *You're cool, Essie. I can't wait to swim with you and hold you in my arms. I really care for you. Let's catch up soon. Ryan.* I pat it in my pocket. I smile—a reference to the fake shark attack—and I know he means he wants to meet me out of school sometime. It's so thoughtful and romantic of him to do that. Any other guy would have just sent a text. The note definitely makes me rise above my problems.

Though I do have far to travel before I can reach the degree of style that Ashleigh has achieved at fifteen. And she's his sister. That's what he lives with, sees, speaks to at breakfast every day. In the light of day, I see I must have imagined the way he seemed on Friday night at Chloe's. He most probably had to stay to take Ashleigh home. Same as me: I couldn't ring Dad to get me earlier as he may have been still at work, and if not, he'd want to know why I wanted to leave. Maybe come in and see for himself. I'd never be allowed to go anywhere ever again. My fingers tingle just remembering Ryan holding my hand.

The beads in the doorway clink as I hand over the stiff brown paper bag. I look up, my retail smile ready. It's Jowan Tallack. I let the smile down a notch.

'Hi, Essie. You finish soon?'

'How did you know I work here?' Not exactly a warm greeting, and I feel bad, knowing my smile would be wider for Ryan.

He shrugs and looks around. 'Merryn told me when I went round.'

Thanks, Merryn. He walks up to the counter. 'I don't have your number and I thought you might like an ice-cream.'

Ice-cream? It's on the tip of my tongue to say I'm not one of his siblings and that I've grown out of ice-cream, but it wouldn't be true.

'You do like ice-cream?' Jowan's staring at me now. We have

the best ice-cream on the peninsula. People even come from nearby towns to have a Jetty Road ice-cream and I haven't had one for ages.

'Yeah, I guess.' I don't sound eternally grateful, but what if someone thinks I'm *with* him? A tiny voice in my head whispers, *does it matter*? Just then Aunty Joy comes out from packing gift boxes in the back room. She sees Jowan.

'Hello,' she says, looking from him to me. Her smile grows wider. See what I mean?

'Jowan's from school,' I say, so she knows he's just a friend.

Her smile doesn't fade. 'Why don't you go then. I'll shut shop.' Her matter-of-fact tone encourages me. Jowan's safe really. If Chloe saw me with him, she wouldn't think I was going out with him. I mean, he's from our class and girls don't usually go out with guys from the same class. Right? On the way out, he helps me drag the shop sign back in.

The ice-cream shop is two doors down. It's an 'Olde Worlde Ice-creamery' where a single-serve is still a two-dollop sky rise. Jowan gets four dollops. A chocolate double-double. So he's a chocolate freak. I ask for a single macadamia-and-English toffee in a waffle cone.

We walk down to the jetty, me trying not to get ice-cream on my fingers as it starts to melt down the cone. There's nothing for it, I have to lick the cone around. We're leaning out over the jetty now in the face of the warm breeze, me swinging my hair back as I keep eating. Not a good place to keep ice-cream in one solid piece.

'It's good seeing you forget everything for once.'

'Pardon?' I must have ice-cream on my chin by now. What is he talking about? By the look on his face, I gather it's some sort of compliment. 'What do you mean?' Do I look weird eating ice-cream?

But he doesn't answer me. Just says, 'Why do you hang around with that mob at school?' He means Chloe and Ashleigh. There are other satellites too. Like me, I guess, revolving round them trying to be part of a group.

'What's it to you?' I don't mean to sound snarky.

An odd look flits over his face. Nothing to take offence at really but it's as if he cares for some reason. 'Wouldn't have thought they were your type.' Surely, he means I'm not their type? It'll take a lot of work, I know, to catch up to Ashleigh for instance. She's almost as impressive as Josephine Reynolds. Wonder if I'll ever have that kind of social grace.

Jowan looks as if he's expecting an answer and actually seems interested. Maybe he does know what it's like trying to belong. Now I think about it, it must be worse for him since he's only new to town. Before I can stop them, surprising words fly out of my mouth.

'At times I feel like the ugly duckling, you know?' Of course he doesn't know. For a moment there's a look of clear horror on his face. Mum hates it too if I say anything disparaging about myself. 'Nothing to do with *ugly* ugly, don't worry.' Interesting how Jowan relaxes. 'Just that the duckling didn't know where his place was, where he was going, who he was.' I don't add the part where no one wanted him. No need to go on a total 'woe is me' campaign.

'*You* feel like that?' There's that emphasis on the 'you' again. But he doesn't know it all. Friday night at Chloe's flicks through my head and makes me cringe.

'Yeah.' I can't tell him about it. Nice Christian girl (so everyone at church thinks) watches soft porn. He'd be so disgusted. See, I don't fit in with anyone. Always on my guard with Chloe and like a mermaid stuck in the desert at church. Now even with Jowan. Like I've said before, I can't work him out. He doesn't follow what Chloe would call the rules of Loserdom.

'But, Essie, you're the swan.'

'Excuse me?' I didn't hear him. Tell me I didn't. Now I do have ice-cream all over my cheek. Gross. Did he say *swan*?

Jowan's stuttering as though he's outraged. 'Th-those girls—they're turkeys—swans would never fly with wild turkeys—it'd be like flying on your own.'

That sounds so sweet, but he doesn't understand. How can I be a swan? You're only a swan when your wings have grown, and you've flown to where you're meant to be. Otherwise, you're flying blind.

I crunch the last bit of cone, resisting the temptation to lick my fingers, while Jowan quits the embarrassing subject of swans. 'There's this youth group I heard about from friends. Friday nights.'

Friends? He's got friends already?

'Would you like to come?'

What is this? A date now? Swans? Now dates? Though I asked for the swan segment, I guess. He sees me hesitating, trying to work out what he means.

'You could come by yourself if you like. Someone will drop you home.' I still don't say anything. *Youth group*?

'See you around, Essie.'

He just leaves me there, thinking in an evening breeze on the jetty. Weird. Friday nights. I don't want to repeat last Friday night, nor do I want to go to a youth group with kids who don't care about the real world. Kids like Jowan. *Swan*? Incredible. Chloe reckons people who don't care what's said about them are dangerous like you have to be part of a group or you disintegrate like a fallen leaf. It sounds logical when she talks about it but, just sometimes, part of me wishes I didn't have to worry about what Chloe thought of me. At times it seems she's in my head like a traffic controller. But I quickly push that traitorous thought aside. What would I do without her? She's right: you do need the support of friends.

Since Dad hasn't answered my text, I think of putting a note on the fridge with magnetic words for him. Like, *waiting for you on the jetty*. But he wouldn't see it. When he opens the fridge he's only thinking of what's inside. *Think again, Essie*.

7

It's been a week since Jowan and I ate ice-creams on the jetty. Weirdness factor: I'm using Jowan Tallack as a marker in time. It's also the same time since I received Ryan's note. That note has given me more confidence. When he smiles at me this morning outside school, I say, 'Hi. How's your training going?' Why else would he be running along our beach when he lives up the coast. He pauses, grins again.

'Great. I have to run 10kms a day.'

I can't believe he's talking to me and just then a few of his mates rock up and he walks on with them. Doesn't look back either.

Then Chloe says this before classes start, 'I think Ryan likes you.'

My heart soars, I can't help it. It's great news. Also, she's in a good mood. Funny how I have a good day if she's feeling happy. I wonder for a split second if this is good and then I push it down when she adds, 'I've seen him look at you.' She seems genuinely interested. 'Has he asked you out yet?'

I'm not sure what to say. There is the note. Was that asking me out? But I don't really want to share the note—it's too special.

Chloe gives a little huff. 'If you can't talk about stuff like this with your best friends, what sort of friend are you?' Now she can tell I'm hiding something; I've hesitated too long. 'I'm sure Ryan would like to hear that you're a good friend and easy to get along with.'

I groan inside. Why is Chloe so interested in my life? 'Well, there was a note—'

'A note!' Chloe smirks at Ashleigh, but Ashleigh's face is unreadable. 'What did it say?'

I don't tell them everything. 'Not much, just that he'd like to see me outside of school, I think.'

'That sounds like a promise of something.' Chloe gives me a high-five, all smiles again. But I feel like I've sold my soul.

At the beginning of maths Chloe suggests another movie night and, Ryan or no Ryan, I don't have the heart for it. I should just tell her why but that will put me right in the middle of Antarctica, all my toes freezing off with no friends to hold my hand. In reality, it leaves me with no sure way of getting to know Ryan better outside of school, but I stay firm.

'Oh, I'm so sorry,' is all I say as I get my iPad out of my bag. I glance up and for a split second, her face contorts into such a naked look of hurt, but then it's gone. Did I imagine it? She's putting her mouth into her 'then change it' shape when I hasten to explain. 'Wish I could but there's something I have to go to.' I make it sound as though my parents want me to do it, a family thing I couldn't possibly get out of. There are a few things in life like that: your father's funeral, for example. I don't say he's died—even though it feels like it at times—but Chloe frowns suspiciously, not even trying to look sympathetic. She knows it must be incredibly serious for me to not go to her house. She's just about to ask when the maths lesson starts. Today, it's a test and if old Crow catches us talking in his tests, it's an instant fail. Even Chloe can see the value of fewer fails on her report.

All through the test, I can feel her anger radiating towards my back and it's difficult to concentrate. I'm shocked at her reaction. It's as if I've put private photos of her online.

Already I feel a boxthorn hedge growing between Chloe and me and I hurry away after class. How can she be so nice to me and then act like this? This is the first time I've ever refused to do anything with her. I can only hope she forgets about it. The odds of that aren't good. I remember what she did to Beth Davey from 10B who challenged her and Ashleigh about smoking in the loo the first week of term. Total excommunication. You could smell the smoke in the lunch shed that day and it wasn't tobacco smoke, but the smell of burning hay at the stake. Poor Beth.

When I get home Chloe messages me. *You're an ungrateful cow. I can't believe after all I do for you that you would treat me like this. What sort of friend are you? Aren't I good to you? How could you hate me so much? What a selfish and spiteful bitch. It's all your fault that I get upset.*

Whoa, that sure came out of nowhere, or did it? The words vibrate before my eyes. It sounds incoherent. I don't hate Chloe. How could she think that? My hands are shaking and a dark dread rises in me that I can't shake off. I've never had anyone say or text anything like that to me. Mum says I'm easy to get along with, that I'm kind and gentle. Even teachers know they don't have to raise their voice to me. Apart from the shock that someone could write to me like that, I've suddenly realised I may never get to spend more time with Ryan. Chloe won't invite me to her house now. She may even say I'm a mean girl. Ryan's sure to hear about it. He'll wish he never wrote the note.

Mum comes in from work. I can't tell her about Chloe's outburst. I haven't even told her about the movie night or how weird I feel lately. Is it just because of the movie night? That was bad enough with dreams of violence. Or is it Chloe too? I'm starting to feel I have to tiptoe around her, so as not to annoy her. Sometimes she's happy, like this morning, but I always seem to offend her. Usually, I don't know what I've done, but I do this time.

I'm still in two minds about the youth group too, but since I haven't been talking to Mum much at all lately, I tell her about it. She's as transparent as an aquarium today. She has different levels, 50 per cent transparency if it's anything to do with people she doesn't know or distrusts—she's never any more cloudy than that—and 98 per cent for church things. Aquarium transparency is right up there. I can even see the gold angelfish in her head swimming in frenzied circles.

'That's so nice, Eseld. Course you should go. Shall I drop you? You can call when you're ready to come home.' She's going to wait around and *be ready* to pick me up? If Mum thinks it's a good idea, then it must be uncool. But there's no way out now. She's clucking like a hen with a dozen warm eggs and I try not to show my exasperation.

Turns out the youth group is in an old deli I've never been into down Jetty Road, but it's been converted to an internet café. MAD Café, it's called. Just what I feel like for coming. Everyone refers to it as The Café. It looks okay at first glance. Kids have milkshakes and coffees. Some are working online. There are even a couple of older guys with guitars playing music you hear on Spotify. None of the kids I've seen so far have antennae sticking out of their foreheads, or wings protruding from their jean jackets. Everyone's feet are firmly on the ground and I let myself relax.

Then I see Josephine talking with Jowan. She swishes that perfect honey gold hair and smiles. A thousand light bulbs go off. She's one of the leaders, I discover. Imagine telling Chloe that the vision at whose feet she worships goes to a church youth group! Then I realise I won't have that satisfaction on two accounts. One, this is my reason for not going to Chloe's house, and on her scales, this won't balance out a funeral. And second, even more importantly, to say I've met Josephine Reynolds out of school hours will take a lot of explaining since they won't believe me. Explaining that will involve where I met her and how come I was there too. I don't even know why I'm obsessing over this. Chloe is not going to talk to me ever again and I don't know how to fix it. Not going to her house will be one thing. To have a faith will definitely compound the issue. Chloe is not warm to Laila and she has a faith. See what I mean?

She might tell Ryan for starters. I'd rather he got to know me first and I tell him in my own way. People have such warped ideas of what Christians are like, hypocrites or controlling extremists. Even *I'm* wary and I'm one myself. Not a good one, I guess, as I have doubts and questions. What a mess. Mum would say 'pray about it', but I feel as if there's a wall between God and me. A great sand dune of porn, booze and rebellious nails. Dad says blessings don't rely on what you do or haven't done, and God loves us the way we are, but lately, that's hard to believe.

'Essie.' Jowan's seen me. Drags me over to Josephine to introduce me. Instantly I'm nervous. A girl who looks like her could be a snob and who'd blame her? Chloe says that good-looking girls have to protect themselves somehow. I cringe. Wish I could get Chloe's words out of my head. Josephine has on blue jeans to die for and a cute top that shows no excess weight and a belly button ring. Brett of the Circuit would be so impressed he'd hold her up as the pinnacle for which we all should strive.

'Hi, Essie.' Her tone is pleasant, genuine. 'Glad you could come.' I smile tentatively. Girls like her can be nasty, a barb coming out like a kitten's sharp claws, also designed to keep people at bay. I wait, but none show. Jowan's not ogling her either. It's as if he hasn't noticed what she looks like.

'Jowan says you're in many of the same classes at school.'

I nod, relieved at how nice and normal she seems. 'Yes.' At first it's hard for me to keep eye contact, but then I realise she's just being kind. I smile. 'I see him down the beach with his brothers and sister too.'

'Do you have siblings?'

'A younger sister, Merryn.' Poor Merryn, I haven't done much with her at all lately. I'm so caught up in my own concerns. Wish I could work my way through it all. Another girl takes Josephine's attention as the music grows louder.

Later, after the group game, the laughing and the singing with the guys—who seem to be able to play anything from rock to jazz—Josephine asks me how I really am. I don't know what to say. How am I really? Happy? Sad? Scared? It's such a mix. I clutch my hot chocolate, start stirring in the marshmallows, and mumble I'm fine. She nods as if I've answered differently.

'It's hard, isn't it?' she says. It's not a real question so I don't comment. 'Keeping it together.' This I understand, and before my brain knows what I'm doing my mouth says, 'Did you feel like that? When you were my age?' How old is she? Eighteen? Nineteen? All that experience.

'Sure. Being a Christian kid isn't the coolest thing to be in school, so difficult not to be a misfit, to just be normal.' She grins as if it's a sad joke. 'I got into some trouble there for a while.' A shadow passes across her face like cloud cover on a hot day and I don't like to ask about it. Then she says this: 'I just had to keep looking for that secret door to the real me.' I stare. *The real her*? It makes me think of the ugly duckling and what I said to Jowan. How could she have ever felt like me?

'There are so many people who want to change us, Essie. And often our worst enemy is ourselves.' It's a weird conversation. I always think I'm the only one who feels the way I do, even though I can't explain, but she seems to understand. It's like a heavy lump sitting on my shoulder has flown off. I still can't put into words what I truly feel, and fortunately, someone else has taken Josephine's attention or she might ask me again. What would I tell her? That I think I'm confused at the moment, maybe a bit sad?' I don't want to say 'depressed', just disturbed by Chloe, disappointed by Ryan. He hasn't followed up on the note yet. There, I've actually admitted it. How hard was that?

I wonder if things might change if Ryan liked me so much he'd want to do some of the things with me that I do. I couldn't take him to our little church, that'd put him right off. But this youth group isn't bad with those guys playing cool music. It's just like a coffee shop, anyone can come in. Josephine's talking to another girl now, quietly, with that warm grace she has. How amazing that she could be so open about her life. As Dad would say, she's sure rocked my boat.

Merryn's in bed when Mum and I get in. Mum's happy I've had a good time. Dad is sitting in the lounge with the TV paused. Mum plops down next to him. Dad asks me, 'How did it go?'

'Good.'

Mum says, 'Jowan was there.'

Dad smiles. He looks a bit sleepy. I'd like to ask them a few questions but they've obviously been having a date night before Mum picked me up and I grin at them. I feel bad sitting with them when I can see Dad's finger hovering over the play button. When I go to my room the TV plays the theme music from *Poldark*. They're both fans.

I try another text to Dad. Surely since he's in the house he'll get it. *Hey Dad, didn't want to disturb you two tonight. How about we have ice-cream on the jetty one afternoon. Love Essie*

I don't say when. Tomorrow's Saturday but he's often working from home on Saturdays if he's here. It's been ages since he and I have done anything special together. Ages since we've sat in our special spot on the jetty. It was like we were drifting on the water in a world of our own. Even if fishermen were on the jetty, they usually fished from the sides. Once a pelican wanting a fish stood beside us thinking we were fishing. He growled with his beak wide open when Dad tried to stroke him. Then he flew off to perch on a lamp post. I loved spending time with Dad but I didn't realise at the time how precious those moments were.

8

Jowan gives me a folded piece of paper on the beach today after school. Ryan's note flies into my mind and for an instant I'm panic-stricken. What if this is a love note—what on earth will I say? But it's nothing like that. The writing is large, more artistic than you'd expect from a farm boy. But it doesn't make sense:

> *My raiment is silent as I tread the earth*
> *or inhabit the dwelling or disturb the water.*
> *Sometimes my trappings and this high air*
> *raise me over the heroes' hall,*
> *and then the strength of the clouds*
> *bears me widely over the people.*
> *My garments sound loudly and*
> *melodiously, sing clearly when*
> *I am not resting on water or land,*
> *a travelling spirit.*

'It's a riddle,' Jowan says. 'See if you can work it out.' He's totally into this Anglo-Saxon poetry. 'There isn't much of it left,' he says. 'All got burnt when the Vikings raided or the Normans took over, which is much the same thing really.' The things he comes out with! Maybe they get more time up north to read.

Maybe they had no Netflix where he lived.

Mum's let me take Merryn this time, as well as the dogs, since I said Jowan often takes his mob down. Merryn's thick with Jowan's sister, Rebecca. I guess the exuberance that Jowan's siblings meet life with would impress a quiet girl like Merryn. I hardly ever know she's around. I bet Jowan's mother can hear exactly what each of her kids is doing at any given moment of the day, except maybe Luke. This is when Jowan starts telling me about the Anglo-Saxon poetry.

'The Exeter Book has all this poetry in it and nearly 100 riddles.' Yep, he'd be just the sort to like riddles. All those fantasy stories have some quest or riddle that has to be cracked by the hero to finish the story or game. 'Some have got such innuendos—you think it's something else for ages and then find out it's a simple thing like a key.' I'm about to ask for an example when I see the colour he's gone. Ah, *sexual* innuendoes. First time I've seen him embarrassed. I grin.

'Wonder what the scribe who copied them out thought about that?' So they had their version of naughty media. 'Why don't you just tell me what my riddle means?'

'There's no fun in that. You've got to work it out yourself.' He doesn't know how frustrated I'm going to get. *A travelling spirit ... raise me over the heroes' hall ...* I sure feel like a travelling spirit at times, flying blind, though that won't help me work it out. I don't read as many fantasy novels as he does. How will I do it?

This time we're on the other side of the jetty. I don't particularly want to be right in front of the Life Saving Club, helping Jowan look after his mob and mine. Though Merryn is never any trouble and I watch her now following Rebecca's leaps into the sea with her own tentative ones while Tyler and Vinny crash around them. Then Jowan comes out with an astonishing statement. He truly surprises me.

'I miss my mare.' He's staring out at the horizon when he says it.

'You have a horse?' This is like a movie. A *horse*? 'What's she like?'

'Pure white. Well, almost. Like the horse that carried Lord Trevelyan off Lyonnesse when it was flooded.' So he likes that story too.

'What's her name?' Knowing Jowan the little bit I do, I bet he's called her Guinevere or Arwen.

'Elaine.' He grins at me, knowing I'll be surprised.

'Elaine?' She hardly had any part to play in Arthur's story and I say so.

But Jowan explains. 'Sir Lancelot was always the model of bravery and fidelity, yet he was the adulterous lover of the queen. I just felt Elaine got the raw deal. She was the Lily Maid who loved him the most.'

'She even died for it.'

'I thought a beautiful mare like mine deserved a pure name.'

I try to think of Ryan talking about poetry or mares and who deserves pure names. Would he know what *pure* means? I open my eyes wide suddenly. Did I just have a negative thought about Ryan? I quickly think of another question.

'You had to sell her?' Maybe that's why Jowan's feeling down.

He shakes his head. 'She's on a neighbour's property at the moment, until we can find stables here to keep her in.'

Imagine having a horse of your own. Incredible. Merryn will set up a shrine to Jowan when she finds out. She reads every horse book she can lay her hands on.

'We all had something big we were allowed to keep when we moved. Desi and Luke wanted their Scott Roxters—we still need to find safe bike tracks so they can ride them. Rebecca wanted the piano—that's okay, so did Dad. Little Tad wanted his swing set. I think Dad knew I'd want to keep Elaine. That's why he did it like that, so it'd be fair. We had to write them on bits of paper and those things didn't go to the clearing sale.'

We're quiet while I'm wondering how it'd feel watching your life being sold piece by piece to people you might not even know. 'Dad had to sell all his pigs.'

'Pigs?' My tone isn't as awed as when he said 'mare'.

'Dad loves pigs,' Jowan informs me. 'Reckons they're more intelligent than dogs. We were too far from the markets to make it work. When he's recouped we might get another place, closer to here, a pig farm. I still like horses and cattle better though.'

'So you'll work on a property when you leave school?'

'Maybe. Something in the country anyway. I'll go to Ag College first and see.'

It's a new world to me. Isn't it incredible what turns some people on? *Pigs.* Me, I've only known the beach, these peninsula towns, school, visiting the city on holidays and camping in the Flinders. You see the rest of the world on TV, but it's not the same as meeting people from it. Chloe may think Jowan's a loser but he has just made me tear up from sympathy.

After dinner, I'm supposed to be doing my English homework but I can't concentrate. I still don't know what to do about Chloe. I try writing a text. It sounds wrong and I keep deleting it, so I write it in Notes first. I hope she doesn't misunderstand. I already apologised when I said I couldn't come, but I try again. That expression on her face when I first said I couldn't come haunts me. *Sorry I couldn't come to your house Friday night. I hope there'll be another time soon. X Essie.*

I do want to get to know Ryan better but that's not the main issue here anymore. Chloe is taking up my whole headspace. I can't stand not being able to make peace with someone. If Josephine were to ask me what I feel right this minute I think I'd say I'm scared. It's horrible knowing I've upset Chloe and I don't know how to make up. Nor do I know how to get her out of my head.

9

Jowan has sure made me think about a few things. I'm even thinking of him on my way down the street to my music lesson, carrying my red leather music case Aunty Joy found at an auction. What would it be like having to pack up your life and live in an alien landscape? Would I cope? Without the sea? I can't imagine life without that expanse of perpetually heaving hills and plains with all its different faces. It can be wild when the wind whips up, at other times so calm the pelicans bob around, fishing. In the evening it shivers over the little stones and shells on its edge like it's trying to make friends. Then some nights, during a storm, you know what a dangerous friend it can be. Like Chloe, I think. Is she dangerous? Or just easily offended? See how easily Chloe sneaks into my head when I'm thinking of something else? It's driving me mad. It's much more peaceful having Jowan in my head so I try again.

Jowan reckons the expanse of the land up north is like the sea too. It has the same feeling of space, of sky meeting with the horizon a long way away. That's why he goes down to the beach so often. He can breathe easier and doesn't sneeze there. Looking at rooftops and fences would make him depressed, he said. That makes me wonder some more. Does Jowan feel depressed? He doesn't look it, but it would be sad leaving the life where you grew up.

When I arrive I sign in at the front desk. The music school is only an old shop converted to music booths. None of which are remotely soundproof, even though you get this false sense of security from the smallness of the rooms. Drums are taught further down the hall from the front desk and music sales. Mrs Mangledorf's room is one of a row, each with a piano. The singing teacher is next door today. I can hear scales. It sounds like a happy child running up and down a hill.

Mrs M sees my nails. 'Eseld, what are those?' I'm tempted to say sweetly, 'Nails', but she wouldn't be impressed, so I keep my mouth shut. 'You will not be able to play in the exams with those. You girls are all the same. No commitment. Always it is what the models do, what the movies say. It is so emotionally immature. It is ...' Momentarily she runs out of steam. I think I might give up music lessons. 'Your talent, it deserves some sacrifices.'

From next door I can hear the words of a song: *even if I lose myself...*

Mrs M sighs. 'Let us see what you can do.' Her 'w's always come out with an extra puff of air. She's right. It's not my best playing.

... with only darkness as my friend. To play fast descents my hand needs to be curled and of course, I can't manage it with my lovely long nails.

'You have shown such promise, Eseld. You have the talent for piano. Not many do.' She's not so angry, more disappointed now, and we do theory instead. Ashleigh says I have such promise in my nails.

... Life is like the sea, waves of loss and of gain. The singing teacher has a beautiful voice. No student would be able to sing with a deep husky tone like that.

At the end of the half-hour, Mrs M leans closer. 'Cut them, Eseld, or I will have to speak to your parents.' I smile and escape her swelling bosom. It only heaves like that when she's upset.

Just as I'm paying at the desk, the door to the singing booth opens. My mouth drops to *my* bosom. It's Mary. She must be taking singing lessons. Sport and music. I wonder how she fits it all in.

'Hi,' she says as she strides to the desk to pay.

'Just started?'

She grins shyly. Her smile is cute. 'Yeah.' It's breathy as though she's just been told a secret. One she's keeping to herself for a while. As we walk outside, I'm feeling uncomfortable about not doing much with her anymore, so I say, 'I'm sorry we don't get as much time together at school like last year.'

She just shrugs. I can't explain to her how Chloe takes up my time at school. She doesn't like it if I spend time with someone else at lunch and yet when I'm with her and Ashleigh, I feel the odd one out.

Mary smiles at me then. 'We can still hang together if we want to.'

I nod hopelessly. I'd like that, but she doesn't understand. I wish I could explain how Chloe is giving me the silent treatment, but I'd feel disloyal. I can't explain anything to Mary and I feel so bad about it.

'See ya,' she says as we go our own ways.

On the way home I check in on Aunty Joy and help her take in her sign. It's on the tip of my tongue to mention Chloe's behaviour to see what I should do, but Aunty Joy has to rush. She and Uncle Bob are going out soon. I'm glad I didn't say anything. If Chloe found out it would be worse. I check my phone for messages but she hasn't answered. Nor has Dad.

Merryn wants some help with her homework when I get in. 'It's my long division,' she starts. I could do with some help too but at least I can do primary school maths. I get us a hot chocolate each and explain how it works. Her face looks a bit tear-stained.

'You okay?' I say. Hope she's not stressed by her maths. That shouldn't happen at her age. Now, I wish Dad could explain a few things to me. Year 10 maths is so complicated.

She shrugs her shoulders. She doesn't let on about much, but I wish she'd say what's bothering her. Guess that's what we're all like in this family. We never hear Mum and Dad discussing their feelings, though they probably do in their room.

'I'm fine,' she finally says. She smiles when she gets the sums right.

'Come on, I'll read to you—what would you like?'

'*Eloise and a Bucket of Stars.*'

'I haven't read that one.'

'It's got horses and unicorns in it. Rebecca lent it to me.'

Sounds like a delightful way to fall asleep. Wish that still worked on me.

After Merryn's in bed, still reading, my mind is at full throttle, as Dad would say. Deep breathing is not helping me relax enough to stop over-thinking my life right now. What do you do when someone who used to really like you, ignores you? It doesn't make sense. And there's been little contact from Ryan lately at school. I'm not sure if the note is enough to keep hope alive. I guess with Chloe not talking to me, which means Ashleigh won't either, I can't expect Ryan to.

And why doesn't Dad bother to answer his texts? Perhaps he only answers business deals.

10

We've been invited to the Tallacks' place for dinner. Merryn actually whinged when she heard. 'Oh please, Mum, can we go, please,' with the 'please' drawn out over five syllables. I consider not going and say so, until Merryn turns the whinge onto me. 'Es-sie.' Then she whispers, 'Dad's going.' And I relent even before Mum gives me her appalled look. She has 90 per cent transparency again today. Uh-oh. Jowan would be on her list of all things wholesome, no doubt. Though Jowan's not boring like I first thought, and no one at school (that's Chloe) needs to know I've gone. I haven't been to Ryan's house even, since Ashleigh's never invited me and not likely to now either.

Mum's icing a cake to take over. 'Mrs Tallack just wants to get to know us, being new here. It's what they do up north—welcome new people into the district by having them for a meal.'

Wouldn't that mean we should be inviting them? Maybe Mrs Tallack knows she'll be waiting until their cattle come home by themselves for town people to think of inviting them to dinner.

Merryn brings her clothes to get dressed in my room. 'Your mirror is bigger,' she says. I change my clothes only once, but Merryn does it too. 'Do I look okay,' she says.

'Of course, you always look okay.' It's odd but I don't think any more about it as Dad calls, 'Let's go.'

The Tallacks are renting and it's not so far from us. Just a few streets and we drive over to save time. On the way, Chloe sneaks into my head again. She's ignored me at school all week. Last Monday I sat on the Lunch Bench before they got there. When they saw me, they went to eat lunch somewhere else. It's disturbing being in someone's bad books. Another text hasn't brought an answer. I'm definitely out in the cold.

'Here we are.' Dad's sounding jovial. Merryn smiles at me. It certainly is a plus having Dad with us.

The Tallacks' stone house has an old-world atmosphere. They have four bedrooms, but it still means Tad has to share Jowan's, who doesn't seem in the least put out about it. When we arrive, Jowan's out in the backyard digging with a pick. He's wearing his Akubra hat and work boots. Mrs Tallack ushers me out to join him.

'You like gardening?' It's hard to see where the dirt ends and his shorts start. Sweat's pouring down his neck, yet he looks pleased to see me. If it were me, I'd be embarrassed to be caught not showered and dressed.

'Not gardening,' he says, and I wonder if I'm going to be told what he's digging for. Treasure? A well? Maybe farmers do weird things like that in a town. I step closer and smell the pungent earthiness of the dirt. It rises to meet me like the salt at the beach, soothing, as if to say: don't think of anything else now, just be here. Just be. I breathe in and slowly let it out. Jowan grins at me. 'The earth works wonders, eh?'

I nod, amazed at how I'm only thinking about being here, not what's happened at school. The beach is like that too—it can whisk away my worries for a time. I almost say what I'm feeling when Jowan speaks again.

'Tad wants a sandpit. Then we'll put rocks round it and Mum will get her rockery as well.' He's doing a good job.

'Did you used to do stuff like this on your property?' Do they dig holes for fence posts?

Jowan grins, he can see what I'm thinking. 'Yeah, helped Dad a lot. Not digging though. We had machines for most things.'

'What did you do?'

Jowan puts the pick down. Guess he knows he's not going to get any more work done now. He sits on a rock. There's one for me too. 'Used to drive the tractor, help with planting, harvesting—that sort of thing. On weekends and after school. Fed the pigs if Dad was busy. Had my own chooks. Bought them as day-old chicks.'

'You had to feed them?'

He nods. 'And collect the eggs, grade them, put them in trays. Then I sold them. That's how I got Elaine.' He must have worked hard. Dad says horses cost a fortune. He told Merryn *he* couldn't even afford one. Jowan's brushing his legs with his hand now. It's relaxing just being here. The sun will set soon and even though we can't see the sea, I can hear it. Birds fly overhead towards the feathery clouds in the west.

'Even though there's a fence, it's still peaceful,' he says watching the sky change colour.

'Yeah.' I'm surprised how worries fall away when I'm with Jowan. Should I ask him about that?

Just then Desi races out to say it's time to eat. We go in, Jowan to the bathroom, me to offer to set the table, but Rebecca's already done it.

Dinner consists of braised steak and vegetables. We hardly

ever have red meat. Jowan's siblings eat dinner with the same enthusiasm they use to jump into the sea. Only Luke has enough space between mouthfuls to notice I haven't had the salt and pepper and he passes it over without being asked. Every now and then he stops what he's doing as though he has to catch up on breaths he's missed. You'd expect a child like that to be self-absorbed, but it's as if it gives him a chance to watch the rest of the world, to think about what his part in it should be. Desi and Rebecca just live. Tad's like them too. Like Pac-Man monsters, they do whatever is in their path to do. I watch Desi shovelling his peas onto his fork. Bet he'd be good at digging a sandpit.

I'm glad Jowan doesn't talk to me at the table. How embarrassing that would be. His parents would think we're together. Already Mum's watching him as though she's conjured him up out of her imagination and she's very pleased with what's she's done. True, I can't imagine Ryan digging a sandpit for a kid—not that he's got any little brothers or sisters—and he groans if he has to take Ashleigh home from school, but he's so interesting. And it isn't just looks, it's the way he wants to keep people safe on the beach, how he talks, how he looks at me as if he likes me. It's only when I'm away from him that I doubt it.

Jowan asks to show me something in his room. I glance at Mum but she doesn't look concerned. We're just friends of course, so nothing to worry about. It's annoying that Mum's most probably making meaningful glances at Merryn. I just hope she doesn't say anything to Mrs Tallack. Jowan's mum looks like the sort of mother who wouldn't get in a fluster. I can imagine there'd be a lot of things she'd think were silly. Like fifteen-year-olds being an item.

Jowan writes poetry. It's all on his computer and I get shown a book he's made himself. He likes desktop publishing. The graphics aren't bad either. One about a leaf is typed in the shape of a tree's shadow.

There's one called Morte d'Arthur. The font's Old English and there's a sword down the left side. 'Tennyson wrote that one,' Jowan says, and I nod. I've read it in English class. The first line is familiar: *So all day long the noise of battle roll'd among the mountains by the winter sea ...*

My finger traces the sword. 'How did Arthur manage it, do you think? To keep going like that when so many were against him?'

Jowan shrugs. 'He knew what he had to do, knew what was best for his country I suppose.'

I'm quiet, thinking about being so sure about a place or cause that you can take up a sword to defend it. What if it meant you missed out on something you really wanted? If Chloe were to confront me about my music or what I think of her movie nights, what would happen? Would I miss out on getting to know Ryan? It's too difficult to think about right now and I hide it deep in my dark pool of impossible puzzles.

Then I notice this enlarged photo of Jowan and his mare. It's on the wall, poster-size above his bed. Elaine has her head turned slightly, half looking back at Jowan, as if she's just shaken her mane for the photo, her front legs slightly apart, graceful. It makes her look as though she's about to bow after a dance. The grace and harmony between them takes my breath away.

Jowan's behind me. 'Beautiful, isn't she.'

I nod, but I can't turn round. The pride in Jowan's words is mixed with a raw longing that I know I'm not meant to notice, and it'll be running wild all over his face. So, out of respect for his feelings, I glance down at his poetry book, still in my hand. That's another thing. Would I show my soul to someone like this? Not likely. How come Jowan knows I won't laugh, or think it's stupid? How come he can say he misses his mare and I can hear the pain in his voice when he talks about her, and I don't know what to say or even how to do that myself: to show what I'm feeling? I wish I could. Then an unwelcome thought appears. Is it true I can't show my feelings? Or do I hide them?

'Hey, Essie, see this?' Jowan is full of surprises. He shows me his sax. Even plays for me. It's really cool. Did I say that? Chloe mightn't say it is, but I know how difficult it is to get a sound out of one, let alone play it well. I let on I play the piano, and he takes me to the family room where their upright piano is. Mine's a full-length portable. Jowan pulls out some music from the stool and, before I know what I'm doing, I'm playing chords, with Jowan on the sax, taking the lead tune.

On the second verse, I can hear a high sound travelling with me. Not a recorder. I glance over my left shoulder. Rebecca's there with a tin whistle. It looks like the real thing, something I've only seen on Irish shows on TV. I give her a grin. She looks like one of the little people that the ancient Cornish believed in. It's a new song for me: 'Maggie May'. Jowan tells me it's a Cornish folksong. Good thing I can sightread, for he puts another in front of me.

Then Rebecca's saying, 'No, this one, this one.' It's called 'Adieu Sweet Lovely Nancy.' All about a young guy going overseas from Cornwall in the old days.

We only get a few bars in and Jowan's father is there singing along from the doorway. Rebecca must have chosen it on purpose to get her father interested. I'm shy at first but then I kind of enjoy it. It's like playing in a band. I've always wanted to do that. We end up playing lots of other stuff like 'The Entertainer', and we jazz it up. Jowan's got some sheet music from Nora Jones' new album and we play that too.

Never thought I'd be saying this but the night at the Tallacks' ends up a success. When we're playing I forget about school totally and feel as if I'm in a different world, where nothing matters except this very moment. At one point when we'd just finished a song with almost as much rhythm in it as rap, breathless from the fun of it, Jowan tells me about a talent quest that's going to be held in April at Jetty Road Tavern. I've seen the sign in the music school too, but who plays the piano in a talent quest? Everyone would be bored, and I say so.

'Not just you,' he says. 'You could play the keyboard, couldn't you? I'd play sax, and we could get Kris and Marty who play at The Café to join us. Maybe one of them can sing.'

'A band. You want us to start a jazz band?'

'Why not? We can make our own sound. Celtic even. Blues is good too.'

I'm half-excited, half-scared to do it. If only Ryan played the guitar and was part of it, I'd know Chloe would think it was okay to do it then. Maybe she'd be friends with me again. Jowan's certainly given me new things to think about.

On the way home, Dad says Jowan is a good lad with his feet firmly on the ground. Mum's little angelfish are glowing after a comment about me having nice friends. Fortunately, she doesn't flog it to death. She and Mrs Tallack have exchanged phone numbers. Mr Tallack actually hugged me on the way out the door and said I have to come back since he hasn't had so much fun in ages. There was something else in his face too, under the smile, like the raw longing in Jowan's voice when he speaks about his mare.

11

Chloe's still not talking to me. For over a week I haven't had a ride home, so this Thursday I again take the bus to our town. Today I'm the last one on, and I see Mary and Laila sitting near the front. I sit behind them and put my bag on the seat beside me. 'Hey,' I say. They both turn and smile. I want to say sorry but the words freeze in my throat. Do they know that Chloe's not speaking to me anymore? Are they also in trouble with Chloe or is it just me? I haven't been to the pepper trees in ages and I still can't talk about it with them.

Then I see their maths homework open on their knees. 'You're doing maths?' I ask.

Mary grins. 'Laila's helping me with the algebra.'

I grab my iPad. 'Can you show me too? I don't seem to understand a thing lately.'

Laila is kind. 'Sure.'

I watch from behind as she explains what we have to do by Monday. I don't think Dad would have explained it as simply. 'Why can't Crow explain it like that?' I say.

Laila laughs. 'I have a big brother in uni who is a maths king. He is very helpful.'

They get off before my town and when the bus stops near the beach, Jowan jumps off right behind me. 'Essie.'

'Hey.' I smile. I didn't realise he was there since I was so absorbed with the girls but he takes it in his stride. I've decided, despite Chloe's warnings about losers, that Jowan is okay. That visit to his place on the weekend was the best fun I've had for ages. I'm wondering if we should start practising music together, but I don't want to be the one to bring it up.

Besides, Jowan's got another idea. 'What do you say we take the kids snorkelling this arvo. Soon it'll be too chilly to do stuff like that.'

I don't even have to think about it. 'Merryn would love it.' So would I. 'I'll text Mum. Meet you down at the rocks in half an hour?'

'Sure.' And we head our separate ways.

Merryn's home already. Mrs Tallack drops her off now if Mum has a shift. 'Snorkelling?' It's the quickest I've seen her get ready. She even knows where the snorkelling gear is. In the meantime, I text Mum. She texts to watch Merryn carefully and I text back that we're going with Jowan and she doesn't text another word, just a kiss.

Merryn's eyes are shining as she scans the rocks. 'It's been so long since we've done this.' She's right, the last time Dad came with us and I can't even remember when that was. Sure enough, Jowan's mob are there already. He is inspiring. I could have been doing things like this with Merryn, if Mum let me, of course. Merryn actually squeals as she sees Rebecca. They do a holding hands, jumping on the spot type of dance. Oh, to be ten again.

When the kids are putting on their masks, I give a few rules that Dad always told Merryn and me. 'Not past the rock that looks like a duck, there's often an undercurrent there.' They all look at the rock I'm pointing at and Luke says it's more like a pigeon. The kids laugh; they're as excited as Vinny waiting for a treat.

Jowan adds, 'If Essie or I say get out now, you all obey immediately.' Even his land-locked siblings seem to know what he's talking about. My 'collision' with Ryan when I thought there was a shark is still in sharp focus in my mind. But I can't think about that now, I need to keep an eye on Merryn or Mum will never let me do this again.

Merryn keeps pace with me in the water and then Rebecca joins us. We locals know this is a good spot for snorkelling since it's further away from where most people swim. We see little crabs, shells, tiny fish. The water's pretty transparent today, like Mum as soon as she knew that Jowan would be here.

Jowan's playing with Tad since Tad's not officially snorkelling like the others. I can see his yellow floaties but not much else of him. He can swim, Jowan says, the floaties are 'just in case'. Jowan heads underwater to show the twins something. Rebecca and Merryn are pointing at things under the water for each other to see. Their joy can be seen in the way they splash, their kicks, the way their heads bob from side to side. Tyler and Vinny would have loved this but I left them home so I could concentrate on Merryn.

Then I hear a squeal or is it a scream? Everyone else has their head underwater, except Tad. He can't keep upright and he's struggling. He's drifted out near the duck rock. I throw myself into the deeper water and swim over like a shark's after me. When I reach him he puts his arms out to me. 'It's okay,' I say. After I hold him up he still doesn't come towards me. He seems to be caught and I can't check. If I let him go, he falls backwards and water splashes over his face, even with the floaties on. I try to see under the water. His flipper must be caught between the rocks and the current is dragging him under.

'Jowan!' But he's right beside me. 'His flipper's caught, maybe slipping lower. Can you dive? I'll hold him up.'

It takes Jowan too long. Tad's crying, saying 'Ow.' What if Jowan can't hold his breath long underwater? I'm wondering if I should join him, shout for Desi to hold Tad, when Jowan springs up gasping and Tad floats fully into my arms.

'Couldn't save the flipper,' Jowan says, 'but I finally got his foot out. I was scared I'd break his ankle.' He looks shaken and we take Tad out to sit on the towels.

Jowan turns to Tad. 'You okay, mate?'

Tad nods and gives a little hiccup.

'Don't worry about the flipper,' Jowan says. 'I'll get it when the tide's out.'

The others finally leave the water to see what's happening, so I get out the chips I've brought for the kids. Jowan sits subdued, watching Tad. He glances over at me. 'Thanks. That was too close.' He hands me the open chip bag. I haven't had a chip all term, but it feels snobbish to not share in eating them.

Jowan's grinning again.

'What?'

'Thanks for the chips too.'

'How come you can swim so well?' I ask him.

He looks at me surprised. 'We're not duffers up north. Our school had a pool.' There's a slight edge to his voice, like it's not a disadvantage to live in the Outback. I'm mortified and quickly apologise. 'Sorry, I didn't mean it like that. I wasn't thinking.' He smiles and I know I'm forgiven.

It's Luke who asks for a story. They're all sitting on their towels like wet birds drying off and the sun is heading down the sky already. 'Jowan tells us stories about King Arthur and the hobbits,' Rebecca says.

'Not at the same time?' I glance at Jowan.

He grins. 'Course not.' I smile back, relieved he's not offended by what I said earlier.

Merryn looks at me expectantly. I haven't told her enough stories lately either. So I tell them the folktale of Trystan and Eseld. Merryn won't mind hearing it again. How the Cornishman, Trystan, was shipwrecked on the coast of Ireland and was saved from the sea by a beautiful girl. 'Even though Cornwall and Ireland were enemies, they fell in love.' Desi pretends to puke. 'As soon as he was well enough to row a boat, she sent him back to Cornwall to be safe. Trystan never knew her name.'

'Is that the end already?' Desi asks.

'No, much later Cornwall wanted to make peace with Ireland, so Trystan was sent to Ireland to ask for the Irish Princess Eseld to marry King Mark of Cornwall. Now Trystan had to fight in a tournament to win the princess's hand for his king. There were many men and many matches, but Trystan won. The princess lifted her veil so he could see her face and his heart sank. She was the very same girl who had rescued him from the sea, the girl he loved. And now he had to take her back to Cornwall to marry his king. At first, she said "let's run away", but he couldn't betray his king who was like a father to him.

'Back in Cornwall, Princess Eseld married King Mark, but although the King was a kind man, she still loved Trystan. She tried not to. Once she and Trystan stole a kiss.'

The boys say 'Ew', even Tad.

'Someone spied on them and reported to the King. They were both put in prison. Trystan wouldn't say a word other than it was all his fault, but Queen Eseld told the king that she had saved Trystan from the sea and loved him before he came to win her to be Cornwall's queen. When he heard this the king was merciful and decided to let them go free, but they had to live far away. Right at that time the Irish army attacked the castle. Trystan wanted to fight. He said, "No one will say that we lost Cornwall because of my love for you, Eseld".' I stopped.

'What happened then?' Luke says.

'It's very sad,' I say. 'He fought so well that he helped save the castle and the kingdom ...' I pause.

'He died, didn't he?' Luke says quietly.

'Yeah, he was a hero,' I say. 'Some folktales are like that. They show how to be honourable rather than get the girl, like in movies.'

Then Rebecca says, 'And that's why you're called Eseld?'

I give her a high five. 'It's one of Dad's favourite stories, even though it's sad.'

The sun is about to sink in a yellow sea. 'Time to go,' Jowan says. We roll up the towels, grab our stuff. Tad climbs on Jowan's back while the others all run ahead of us, just like Tyler and Vinny.

Telling that story makes me even more determined to get Dad's attention. I'm so annoyed he's not responding and he's still not home from work tonight, that I decide to ring. A woman answers. 'Yes?' She doesn't give her name.

'Um—' I'm totally flummoxed. 'But this is my dad's number.'

'I'm sorry, I can't help you,' she says. I can tell she's about to hang up, but she hesitates. 'Was that you sending texts about a jetty?'

'Yes.' My mind is whirling. What on earth is going on?

'Well,' the woman says, 'this is my phone, so please stop

sending texts.'

I hang up and write Dad an email.

Hey Dad, I've been texting you and you haven't answered. Is everything okay? Love Essie.

There has to be a logical explanation.

12

Today in English, Chloe is staring at me strangely. It makes me want to check I haven't tucked the back of my skirt in my underpants by mistake. But at least she is looking at me. It's been almost two weeks since she's made eye contact. It seems she's talking to me again. She invites me to sit with them at lunch as if the last twelve days haven't happened. Nor does she apologise. I don't have much to say on the Lunch Bench. What if I put my foot in it and get frozen out again?

Ashleigh's talking about the movies at the drive-in. Can I imagine Mum and Dad letting me go to the drive-in? Not likely. But Ashleigh never lets parental disapproval interfere in the things she needs to do. She just doesn't tell. Her motto is, 'What they don't know, doesn't hurt them.' I'm thinking about the things I did on the weekend and try to decide which one would make cool conversation. Dinner at Jowan's? Snorkelling with him yesterday? Chloe would look at me in disgust and say, '*That* loser?' Like there are quite a few we need to steer clear of and how could I have been so careless. A talent quest mightn't do the trick either.

Ashleigh stops to take a bite of celery, and Chloe asks me

how my weekend was. She sniffs after I say I didn't do much, then, with an effort at casualness she stirs up my whole day. 'Ryan wants your phone number.'

I nearly choke on my sandwich. *Finally*. He could even have asked me for it. Mary would say I don't need a match-maker, that I could just walk up to Ryan myself. But I know how things work between year levels. Often a guy will ask a friend to organise a meeting with a girl from a different year.

'Shall I give it to him?' she asks with a sidelong glance at me. A few weeks ago she would have grinned slyly. But today I can tell she thinks I don't deserve Ryan's favour. She may be right, I even *feel* boring today. I have nothing to say that doesn't involve Jowan Tallack, music, the beach, dogs or youth group. Or Exeter riddles. Help. I wish I could rise over this pepper tree like whatever it is in that riddle. *By the strength of the clouds.* What could it be? A feather? A raindrop? An angel? Which brings me back to Ryan. Is this real? Does he finally want to spend some time with me?

'Sure.' I try to sound as though it's no big deal. It may not have been the right tone to use. Maybe it shows I'm not grateful. Chloe is still not smiling. 'You know, Essie, kind and sensitive people are boring and can't think for themselves. They never get anywhere, don't stand up for themselves and don't tell the truth.' She's looking straight at me and I don't think she's joking. 'Do you want Ryan to have your number or not?'

It's hard to get my mouth to work. 'Of-of course I do. Thanks for letting me know.' She smirks at me while I try to keep my face from crumbling. Why do I feel so bad? Or is she right—am I too sensitive?

Ashleigh doesn't seem to notice any tension and starts planning for our English excursion. 'We'll be going with the

Year Elevens,' she says. 'Ryan's going too, of course.' Not a look in my direction. It's as if she doesn't realise I like him.

I feel Chloe's gaze on me again. *Careful, Essie.* Does she think I'm not one of them after all? I look up and smile, trying to trim down the boxthorn hedge. Wish I could tell her about Josephine Reynolds, now that would save my skin. Goss is what thaws Chloe out any time, but I can't tell without blowing my cover. Chloe would want to know everything, getting out her shovel, digging the earth over, like Jowan's sandpit, until my life wouldn't be my own.

This is when I see Mary. She doesn't always sit with us due to sports practice and in one second I've done it: I tell Chloe about Mary learning to sing. Fortunately, it's such a shock she doesn't ask how I know. I forgot I'd have to disclose my piano lessons.

'You're kidding!' Chloe's eyes burst alight as if she's a vampire invited to the giraffes' house. Her bloodlust unnerves me. I have a vision of Mary being tied ankles and wrists to a basketball pole, hay at her feet, ready to be lit. When the flames start it will be my fault. Mary will look at me, confused, her eyes asking, *Why? What did I do to you?* How would I explain? That I was just trying to survive? Yeah right. I hate myself.

'What a nerve,' Chloe says with a wicked-queen snicker. 'Fancy *her* trying to excel in that.'

I shift uncomfortably on the bench. I shouldn't have said a thing, it sounds so much worse, repeated in the open air, metallic, sharp and programmed for impact. I've sacrificed Mary's shy secret to a girl I need to keep as my friend but why? I wouldn't have said this last year. Why now? How have I morphed into someone so vile in less than a term? Jowan would never understand what I have done.

'What will you wear on the excursion?' I ask, trying to divert the disaster I've set in motion. 'What to wear' is usually Chloe's number one concern, but it doesn't work this time. She chooses not to hear.

'Like, why doesn't she get the weight off anyway?'

This is where I should say Mary is not overweight. It's them who are too thin, but I'm shaking inside. I'm scared, but I don't know what of and that makes it worse.

'Puffs up the stairs,' Ashleigh adds. 'Well, I don't feel sorry for her at all.' She spreads her uniform down her flat stomach. 'It takes work to get into shape, but like, anyone with a milligram of willpower and character can do it.' How can she say that when Mary plays sport? It's like they're talking about someone else.

All I can think of as I watch Mary walk closer is the cute smile at the music school, that look on her face just like Merryn's the day she did her first somersault.

As Mary strolls past, right in front of us, Chloe doesn't miss a beat. She sings a scale. 'A-a-a-a-a-a-a-a. You need style to look good singing, not footy boots.' Chloe and even Ashleigh fall all over the bench, laughing. Mary doesn't turn and look, but are her steps just a little more pronounced like she's pushing through thick mud? That's threatening to suck her down, engulf her at any second?

I want to run after her, but if I do, that's what will happen to me. Frozen out. And Ryan won't get my number. Is that what Chloe's trying to do? To show me I need to toe her line?

Merryn's in bed, reading probably, and I'm doing maths homework by myself. I wish Dad would answer the email. I could ask him about this new set of algebra questions. At least I passed that last test on the day Chloe had her fit, but only just.

I've heard that musicians are often good at maths. That theory passed me by. I wonder how Jowan finds maths. Schoolwork is not what we talk about, but it makes me think of what it must have been like for him in a much smaller school where he would have known everyone. They may have lived up near where we used to go camping years ago in the Flinders Ranges. That was so much fun. We climbed Mary's Peak, walked bush trails, Dad told jokes and cooked barbecues for us every day. Mum and Dad were so relaxed. They told yarns of their childhoods around the fire, Cornish folktales too. That was Dad. But the best thing, which I didn't fully appreciate at the time, was just spending time together.

I get into bed and try not to think about why a woman would say Dad's phone is hers. It's just weird enough to make me not ask him or Mum about it. What if I make trouble by asking?

13

Much Ado About Nothing in the Town Square finally arrives. A Shakespeare troupe from Adelaide is touring country towns so we don't miss out on culture. I don't think we miss out on much, actually, I feel sorry for people who can't look at the sea each day. But it's still exciting. We don't have to wear our uniforms and I get dressed at least three times. Merryn watches me and says what she thinks is best. But her ideas are too tame for a Year 11 guy. In the end, my top and the skirt I usually wear to church will have to do. Ryan raids my thoughts as I put on my make-up. He did finally ring me yesterday, a whole five days after Chloe must have given him my number, unless she forgot. Or did she wait on purpose? Would she still be paying me back for not coming to her house?

On the Lunch Bench today, Chloe wanted to know everything about the call. It's like she lives her life through me. 'He said, "Hi,"' I ventured, not wanting her invasion. Nor did I want to let on that the call was so short I wondered if something was wrong. But maybe I'll need some help later. She does understand him, and Ashleigh is his sister. Though lately, all Ashleigh can think about is Brett.

Chloe clucked her tongue. 'And?'

'He just wanted to know if I was going on the excursion this evening.'

She seemed satisfied with that, as though she was just checking I wasn't getting above myself. It's hard reading all the right cues. At times I think I'm dyslexic when it comes to working out what Chloe wants. It seems like she says one thing one day and changes it the next. But Jowan Tallack? What you see is what you get. Surprises, but not nasty shocks. Though Ashleigh says there's no gain without pain. Maybe Jowan isn't in the running because he's not hard enough to get to know? Oops, that sounded just like Chloe's voice. I think about that some more. Is she in my head so much I'm starting to repeat her words? I truly do not want to sound like Chloe, so what am I doing? Why do I stay being friends with her? It's not just Ryan; there's something else and it's plaguing me. Why do I keep gravitating towards Chloe even though I feel like I'm walking on eggshells, trying not to upset her?

Our classes are taking buses from school to the park since it's a school trip. Chloe and Ashleigh always sit together so that leaves me finding another seat. Mary walks by but I ignore her gaze. I'm still too mortified to smile at her. Jowan glances at my empty seat an instant as he passes and I hold my breath, but fortunately, he's caught on that I don't want much to do with him at school. If I see him down the beach, fine. He seems okay with it, doesn't get shirty over it like some would. Guess he thinks it's a good idea too. Kids at school do come to the wrong conclusion as soon as you talk to a guy. It wouldn't matter if it was Ryan of course, but he doesn't sit with me either. All the Year Elevens bag the back of the bus and I can hear him with his friends, laughing. It sounds like a joke we 'poor Year 10s' wouldn't understand. I didn't tell Chloe the rest of Ryan's short phone conversation about how he hoped we could sit together in the park. I wonder if he's forgotten he said that.

'This seat taken?' It's Beth Davey. I hesitate, Chloe and Ashleigh are two seats behind me, but what the hell. There aren't too many seats left and she'll have to sit somewhere. Surely Chloe has stopped thinking about Beth's objection to them smoking in the loo at the beginning of term.

'No,' I say, sliding over. Beth's cut her hair. It looks nice, a French style, short and wispy around her face. It suits her. Maybe I should tell her, but I don't. She might think I'm sucking up, trying to make amends for hanging around with Chloe and Ashleigh.

'Have you read the play?' she asks.

She's not in my English class so she wouldn't know the preparation we've been through with Ms Bower. I nod. We even saw the film to fill in the bits we didn't understand in the text.

'Which part did you like best?' She's just making conversation but I guess we have to start somewhere.

'Um. Hard to tell. The bit where Beatrice and Benedick get tricked into saying they love each other?' That'd be cool if it happened to Ryan and me. 'No, maybe the bit where Benedick says he'll do anything in the world for Beatrice.' I don't add I wish someone would do that for me.

Beth smiles. 'I like the part where Claudio is about to marry the other girl and finds out it's Hero after all.'

Chloe said 'sucked in' when we read in class that Claudio had to marry another girl to make up for 'killing' Hero by saying she wasn't a maiden. Funny how in those days it was the biggest insult ever to have your virginity doubted and now we have to keep it quiet or we're laughed out of class.

Beth makes it sound as if things turn out for the better if you try to make amends like Claudio did. I look across at her. She gives me a grin, wary, as if she's a wild possum standing a long way away just in case. No doubt she knows I'm friends with Chloe who hates her, but I don't want to hate anyone. Close up Beth doesn't seem bad at all and I smile back. Since she lives in the next town up the coast and is in a different class I had no idea we had things in common. By the time we get to the Town Square we've worked out we both like running along the beach—she's got dogs too, blue heelers—and I've invited her to the youth group barbecue at the beach on Friday night. My mouth sort of did that before I'd thought of any consequences, but it should be safe. Beth's not about to be talking to Chloe.

Ryan still doesn't make a move as we get off the bus. He glances my way and smiles. He hesitates and it looks like he's going to talk to me but one of his mates drags him forward. 'C'mon, let's get the top seats.' So frustrating, he obviously hasn't told his mates he likes me.

That's when Jowan walks up beside me. 'You okay, Essie?'

'Sure.' And I catch up to Beth.

Ms Bower and old Crow—who's come to help—tell us where to go. For one horrible moment, I think they're going to make us march in rows. I bet Crow's capable of it. When he started teaching they would have still been caning kids for reading a word wrong. Beth walks with me and I hear Chloe and Ashleigh murmuring behind us. We get directed to tiered seating that's been set up on the grass under the old pine trees. I'm glad Beth stays with me for Chloe and Ashleigh seem to have forgotten I'm here. Ryan's playing it cool too, but I don't mention that to Beth. Maybe nothing will come of it, and how embarrassing would that be, explaining why.

It's growing dark, medieval music begins: recorders and flutes, even a lute. Then Beatrice, with Hero and her dad, walk onto the grass in front of us. I've never been so close to a theatrical cast before. There are lights set up in the trees and on tall frames; the costumes are exciting. I'd like a dress like Hero's to run along the beach in at dusk. It'd look good draped over a white horse too. Things like that I could never say to Chloe.

Even though I'm nervous about Ryan and whether I've forgotten what he'd said about where to meet, (as if), I still manage to catch most of the play. How exciting it would be if Ryan said something like Benedick does: *I do love nothing in the world so well as you. Is that not strange?* And he asks Beatrice to bid him do anything for her to prove his love.

I love that word, 'bid'. Could I bid Ryan do a task for me? It was a dangerous thing for Benedick to say for she asks for Claudio's life. Is that true love or not? To do absolutely anything for the beloved?

What would Ryan do for me? Would I do anything for him?

Beatrice doesn't let Benedick get away with mere words: *But for which of my good parts did you first suffer love for me?*

I'd like to ask Ryan that too.

Benedick replies: *Suffer love—a good epithet. I do suffer love, indeed, for I love thee against my will.* Beatrice isn't pleased but I know what he means. It's painful, liking someone, wondering if they like you too.

Then just as Benedick's saying: *Serve God, love me and mend,* I feel something sharp land on my back. A twig off the tree? A little stone? I look around and I see Ryan below me under one of the pine trees. I climb over Beth, whispering that I'll be back.

Fancy leaving it until near the end before making contact? I feel like telling him so. What was that phone call about, if not to sit together tonight? The disappointment wells up, but when I get close to him my tongue freezes. He's even better looking than the actor playing Benedick. What do I do now? I can't remember what I was going to tell him. *Talk, Essie. Make conversation.*

'Essie.' He bends towards me.

I can't believe the Mad Mouse momentum I suddenly feel. My insides lurch forward as my pulse takes off. My stomach manages to stay behind and flutters around. It's a dizzy feeling having all your innards separated like that. It's hard to breathe, hard to say anything. Ryan doesn't notice only half of me is there.

'Glad you came, Essie.' I still haven't managed to say a word, especially about why we weren't sitting together, for he steps closer. 'You look so cool tonight.' Are these sweet words to the ear or what? I forget about my earlier disappointment and smile.

'Thanks,' I manage, trying to think of what to say to keep him talking, to get to know him better. We haven't had many conversations and there isn't much time before the play will finish. And that's when he kisses me. It's totally out of the blue. At first, I feel as if I'm under the water, a breaker has just hit me and I'm swirling around trying to surface, but then I get used to it. The wave has passed and I take steady strokes across the bay. When it stops and I've come into shore, he says, 'See you around. Okay?'

My mind is saying, *Wait, that's it?* But I can't get my mouth into gear. What's the hurry? But I guess I can understand. He's with his Year 11 mates, he can't come and sit with me. The audience starts clapping and I nod uselessly as he slips back to his group.

All I can think of now as I make my way back to Beth is that my lips are no longer virgin lips. I have been kissed! By Ryan Kitto!

14

Being kissed should make me feel different. That's what I thought, but I don't, and shouldn't the guy talk a bit first? At least he could say something momentous like *I can't get you out of my mind* or *You fascinate me, Essie. I've been dying to go out with you since I saw you at the beach that day.* Just to repeat what he wrote in the note about caring for me would be better than the nothingness I received in the shadow of the pine tree. Though Ryan must like me, or else he wouldn't have kissed me in the first place. Maybe he's just shy, though he doesn't look it. Maybe that's why he doesn't talk much. Or why he hasn't rung again or spoken to me more at school.

I'm saying all this to the face in the mirror, as I put my make-up on. Tonight's the barbecue at the beach. I make sure I use waterproof mascara, just in case we end up in the water. At least it's near the next jetty so there's no fear of Ryan seeing me while he's on duty at the Life Saving Club.

The doorbell rings and Mum lets Beth in. Mum puts on her extra-mile smile That makes me look at Beth a bit closer. She has a bikini on under that top and her shorts are the latest from Rip Curl. Her towel—a proper beach towel, not a bath towel like

Jowan's—is in a cloth bag slung over one shoulder as though she doesn't remember it's there. She looks great.

Mum doesn't smile at Chloe like this. Not that Chloe has ever visited my house, but if we see her down the street, Mum's politeness is basic, no extras. A traitorous voice in my head says that's because Chloe is only interested in her own agenda, not my mum, but I try to ignore it.

'Hi, Mrs Pederick.' Maybe that's it: Beth is actually making eye contact with Mum. It's just the sort of thing adults like. It makes Mum feel safe, and her transparency level rises. It must be heartening to Mum that I've found a friend at last who'll go to youth group, but Beth hasn't been yet. She might hate it. It's nerve-wracking. If she does hate it, who will she tell?

'Do you have everything, Eseld?' Mum's going to go on about me taking my mobile and what ride I'm getting home, so I head her off at the back door. 'Got everything. Bye.'

Outside, Beth grins. 'So that's your name. I thought it might have been Esther.'

'Wish it was sometimes. Esther I could cope with, but Dad loves the Cornish folktale, "Trystan and Eseld". I've been brought up on Celtic folktales, plus he had a great aunt called Eseld.'

'I've got my grandmother to blame for mine. Don't know why parents don't try to be more creative.'

I chuckle. Mine thought they were. Maybe Beth and I should swap. I wouldn't mind an ordinary name: not so much to have to live up to. People would see 'Beth' written on an interview sheet and think, this person will be boring, and then you walk in and give them a surprise. Eseld is definitely hard work.

Jowan sees us and waves as we dawdle over the sand dunes. The sun's behind him, low on the horizon. Soon it will spread all those red and orange feathers. Josephine is there, playing social cricket and laughing when she hits the tennis ball. A guy is already cooking sausages on a portable barbecue plate. Jowan seems to be helping. The breeze blows in off the sea. Sea, salt and seared meat is an interesting combination, makes you hungry. Beth is carrying her sandals. I take mine off too and enjoy the feel of the sand, still warm beneath my feet.

There's a pile of kids I've never seen before. A few of the guys are what Chloe would call geeks like her brother. I check Beth out, but she doesn't seem to have noticed and we join the fielding team. With this game, everyone's on the fielding team unless you're batting. Good thing I didn't bring the dogs. Vinny would get hold of that ball and never let it go. It's my turn to bat. The guy who's bowling looks familiar; he's tall with curly black hair, older than Beth and me. He grins. 'Ready?'

I nod and he runs towards me and lets loose the ball with a grace Len McGrath would be proud of, as Dad would say. I actually hit it. Not far, but far enough for Josephine and me to get a run. No one seems to be counting, it's just for fun. We laugh as we pass each other. Then Josephine bats but she hits a dolly. The bowler catches it easily and she's out. It's Beth's turn. Another guy wants to bat but the bowler says, 'No. Beth just came, and we should be fair.' It's all so polite.

Not so polite, however, when the food's ready. The younger guys start jostling the table that's been set up. 'Hey,' calls the guy who's been cooking. Turns out he's the youth pastor at the church that started up The Café and his name is Oliver. 'Girls first tonight.'

There are groans behind us while we girls all take pieces of bread with a sausage or chop. I choose a sausage. Chops are far too difficult to eat in public. I'm squirting mine with the tomato sauce when I see the curly-haired guy say 'Hi' to Beth. And suddenly I remember where I've seen him before. He plays guitar in The Café. Jowan comes over then and I ask him. 'That's Marty, isn't it?'

'Yep. Kris is here too.' He points him out. 'There he is, with the mustard. He plays bass. Kris can sing too.'

'You've already asked them?'

Jowan nods as he takes a mouthful of lamb chop. Don't know how guys can do that. I'd rather not eat if there's a chance I'll get caught with meat between my teeth. Maybe it's because we don't have it much at home.

'What did they say? Did they think it's a stupid idea?'

'Nah. They can't wait till we start practising. They're both in Year 12 though. Marty reckons they won't have much time, but he says he'll still do it, even if he can't make all the practises. Kris too.' I take another look at Marty. He seems to like Beth and she doesn't look grossed out. Guess she'll want to come with me again then. I sigh. If only Ryan would like to come. If I could only get to know him better, I'm sure he would.

Jowan walks back to Marty and it's right then as I take a bite of sausage that it happens. Ryan jogs past. He has to swerve, for the barbecue is set up fairly close to the water and he's jogging on the hard sand, but he doesn't slow down. Nor do I think he's recognised me. After all, I do have a sausage and bread in my face. I stare after him, watch his suntanned legs disappear into his white sneakers as they eat up the beach. I had no idea he jogged so far when he trained.

'You know him?' Josephine is behind me. I'm about to shake my head, but what's the point here?

'Yes,' I say, 'but I think it may be a hopeless cause.' Lately, I feel like the Lady of Shallot, poor Elaine pining for Lancelot.

Will Ryan ever contact me again? Just a kiss. It doesn't make me feel so good about myself right now. Josephine leads me away to sit by ourselves. No one seems to notice or care, especially not Beth. Jowan's talking to Kris now, about music most probably.

'Essie, you won't like me saying this I guess, but guys aren't the ribbon at the end of the race.' I just stare at her. What's she getting at? That Ryan's not my type? If a girl at school said that to me, I'd be hurt. Though Chloe has come close. It seems different coming from Josephine. She sounds as if she knows what she's talking about and then she proves it.

'I just wouldn't like to see you do something stupid like I did.' I bet my eyes widen. 'Stupid' and 'Josephine' do not belong in the same sentence together.

'When I was sixteen I had a boyfriend. I should have stood up to him, but I did things I didn't want to. Guess it affected me in a strange way—I ended up with anorexia and a stay in hospital. When I got better I changed schools, made a new start, but I'll always have to be careful. About the anorexia.' She has that look on her face now that Chloe thinks is disdain and she tries to perfect it, but now I know what it is. It's sadness for what she's gone through.

'How did you—?' I'm meaning how did she get through it, but she seems to know.

'When I was in hospital, Oliver was the chaplain for the youth ward.' We both look over at him joking around with some of the kids. He'd be cute if you were twenty. 'He told me some things. He thinks some kids have such a hard time because they don't have faith.' She pauses, finding the right words and then goes on as though the ones she's got will have to do. 'It was like God tapping me on the shoulder. "Come dance, Josie," he was saying. "It's you I want to dance with, it's you I love".'

'Really?' This should sound weird, but Josephine is so genuine that I want to hear more. 'What happened?'

Josephine smiles. 'I joined the divine dance.' Then the smile fades a bit. 'I wish I could say believing in God makes life easier, but it doesn't always. Tough things still happen. There isn't always what we call a happy ending. My boyfriend didn't understand that I wanted out of the type of relationship we had.'

'He dumped you?' A guy didn't want Josephine?

She nods. 'I realised he didn't want the real me, he just liked how I looked. He enjoyed how the guys on the street stared at him when we were together, but he never once tried to find out what was in my head.'

I'm trying to work out where all this might be heading. Would Ryan be like that? Surely not. I push his hurried kiss out of my mind. 'I've always been a part of everything—church, family, now youth group, but it's still hard,' is all I say. What I really mean is, it's so hard not to doubt it all, but I don't tell. And then there's Chloe. And Dad—I sigh.

'In one way it's easier for me, Essie. I can remember what it was like before. I don't have a Christian family and even though Mum thinks I've lost a screw, she's pleased I'm happy and not unwell anymore.'

'I don't know anything different, perhaps that's why I find it's so easy to get side-tracked—there's no blinding light, no taps on my shoulder, to remind me who I am.'

Josephine stares out at the sea. There's a fishing boat gliding out for the night. When she turns to face me she hits me with this: 'Essie, do you want to wake up at forty and find you're still buried under what you think everybody else wants you to be?'

Why does she think I do that? How does she know? Josephine puts her hand over mine. 'Dance, Essie, lift your wings. Dance to *your* tune, not to theirs.' She's talking as if she knows my every waking moment.

At times I feel like I'm a songbird that's sat on a frozen pond too long and my wings have stuck there. Then the ice melts and I'm pulled here and there, losing the beat, finding it again, only to realise I'm in a different song altogether. Can I ever find my original tune? What if I don't remember what it was? And right now there's no way I can explain this to Josephine.

When I arrive home, Dad's in the lounge. 'Hey, Es, did you have a good time?'

I nod.

'Thanks for your email.'

I sit on the couch. 'Is everything good?' I can't say what tries to push into my mind.

'Sure.' There are more lines around his eyes and dark patches underneath. But I ask anyway. 'Why didn't you answer my text messages?'

His face is blank. 'I didn't get any from you.'

So it must be true—he's given his phone to another woman.

15

School sucks again. Ashleigh never mentions Ryan to me personally, and it makes me wonder if he's said anything disgusting about me. Maybe I was supposed to kiss him back and show some interest. But I was pretty gobsmacked at the time. Ashleigh's saying how Brett wants her to go away for the weekend to a beach shack his parents own. What am I doing on this Lunch Bench? I can hear Josephine in my head. *I wouldn't want you to do something stupid.* But I can't say that to Ashleigh. She acts like she knows everything. But what if Brett doesn't really care for her, like that guy Josephine knew? I can't say anything without giving away Josephine's life story. Not after what I said about Mary. And imagine the fallout. 'You go to a *youth group?*' Chloe might give me the cone of silence again. I'm getting tired of having to double-think Chloe's thoughts first, so I can interpret my own. Didn't I have a point of view before Chloe took an interest in me?

Chloe's talking about The Club behind the pub now. Everyone calls it *The* Club as if it's the only club on the peninsula. Maybe it is. She wants us all to go. I say I'll think about it. Ashleigh frowns at me like she's caught on I'm scared of my parents' reaction. But imagine how red in the face Dad would get if he found out. Dad doesn't say much to me during the general course of a day, he's so busy at his work, but do something stupid or dangerous and man, would he notice that.

'Of course, we can always ask someone else, but we thought you might be interested since Ryan will be going.' Ashleigh lets his name hang in the air and I catch Chloe's smirk. It's the first time she's mentioned Ryan's name to me directly.

I reach out and take the bait. 'I'll check what I've got to wear.'

It's the sort of thing Chloe says when she's seriously considering going out. They sit back, start talking about Brett's beach shack, and I decide I need to get books out of my locker.

Mary is in the locker room. She glances at me and I'm so embarrassed, I pretend I don't see her. But Mary surprises me. 'Are you going to the music school's soirée?' she asks.

Does she have to remind me? Those soirées are so boring. Held in the RSL Hall with a piano that saw better days before World War 2 and little kids getting up, excited to play 'Twinkle Twinkle Little Star'. All so we have a chance to learn to play for an audience. Even the word 'soirée' sounds nineteenth century. I try to make an effort. It's a wonder Mary still talks to me after that day when Ashleigh and Chloe baited her about singing. She must know I was the one who told them.

'Yes.' I haven't worked out how to get out of those soirées yet. 'Will you be singing?' I try to sound neutral and Mary gives the cute smile I saw at the music school that Saturday. She nods. She looks happy and I hope it goes well for her on the night. Her kindness encourages me to have a go at apologising.

'Um—that other time, at lunch. I'm really sorry. I was only

making conversation. I'm sure they didn't plan to treat you like that.'

'It's okay, Essie, you don't have to make excuses for them. I know you don't mean to be like them.' Then she walks out.

I'm standing there staring after her. What was she getting at? That I don't mean to be like them? I guess I have been trying very hard to be *liked* by them and if you are like them, you get their approval and know you're fitting in. If you're like Chloe, you care about how you look and what is the right thing to do. You get a cool boyfriend like Ryan. I do have her voice in my head too much lately but I never meant to be Chloe's clone— just wanted to survive.

After school Merryn and I take the boys for a run down on the beach. Mum's totally eased up on that one, to Merryn's relief. I don't leave it until after dinner anymore. The sun's setting earlier and I love that time of day. Everyone's on their way home including the seagulls, and there's a hush. Even the sea is quieter, as though the sun is an emperor to bow to before it hides from view.

Merryn's running ahead with Vinny. Tyler pretends to be more sedate, being older, but soon he won't be able to resist the water. At least Merryn gives me lots of space to think. I doubt Jowan's brothers and Rebecca would give him much space in his head, except Luke maybe. I'm thinking about what Mary said. Josephine too. Do I live my life to please others? I don't think I do with Jowan, but why do I always bend to what Chloe wants? Because she can be nice and make me feel wanted and I want her to show that affection to me again? Do I feel sorry for her? I've never met her olds. I can't even imagine them as she's never mentioned them. Or do I not want to miss out on a chance to get to know Ryan? What I do know at the moment is how nervy and unsure I feel when I'm with her now, and I'm still not certain why.

Then I remember what Jowan said on the jetty about Chloe and Ashleigh. Seems ages ago now. Said they were turkeys. I was shocked at the time, almost scared they'd know in some way what he said. It should be funny, but I feel disloyal grinning about it. Sacrilegious. There are girls in our class who'd have a go at him if they knew he'd said that, let alone Chloe letting loose her freeze-out treatment. But it wouldn't work on him, would it? You can only be frozen out of a group you want to be a part of. If you don't care, it doesn't mean anything.

'Hey Essie!' *Ryan?* I turn, smiling.

Not Ryan. Jowan. He's by himself for once. 'Mum's got the others down the street,' he says to Merryn. I hope my smile hasn't dropped too much, then I notice his face is flushed and his eyes are bright.

'What's up?'

'Dad's found a stable. They billet your horse and you can go there any time to groom her and take her out for exercising.'

Merryn squeals and I grin at him. It's hard to resist sharing another's happiness. 'When will this happen?'

'On the weekend. Dad and I are going up on Saturday to bring her down. The stable's not far. I'll be able to give Elaine runs on the beach.'

'That's so cool, Jowan.' I actually mean it and he's looking at me as if it's the first time I've ever spoken to him.

'You can ride her one day too, if you like.' It's quietly said but I sense what he's offering. It would be a big thing for me to let someone outside the family take the dogs for a run.

'I've never ridden her. She'd know, wouldn't she?'

Jowan smiles. It's a nice smile too. 'She'll manage. She even puts up with Tad.'

'Me too?' Merryn jumps on the spot and Jowan laughs.

'Of course.'

She runs off so the dogs will chase her.

I'm just thinking how easy it is to talk with Jowan when the conversation gets round to the guys who are going to play with us in the talent quest. 'Where shall we practise'?

'The Café. It will be perfect.'

I'm quiet, thinking about anyone being able to walk in and hear us. That would be nerve-wracking.

'It'll be like a jam session,' Jowan says, 'and kill two birds with one stone. It'll give background music to The Café.'

'Maybe if we come a bit earlier and start before people come in,' I suggest.

Jowan's happy with that. Guess it won't be so hard on Marty if we can fit it in with times he's already there. It's not long before Jowan asks me what I think of The Café.

'It's a good idea,' I say, not mentioning how I once thought it might be a deadhead den. 'Better than our tiny, historic church,' I add with a grin.

Jowan grins back. 'The church here is more dated than ours up north. The Café is pretty cool though.' It's the first time I've heard Jowan say the word 'cool'. Guess that sooner or later you start learning the language of the people you live with. He doesn't say g'day anymore like his dad still does.

We're walking along the beach now. Merryn's happy with the dogs but she's a bit further in than usual. Maybe all that time spent with Rebecca has made her more adventurous. 'Not too far, Merryn.' I sound like Mum and I cringe.

Jowan's grinning.

It's almost dusk, and I choose this moment to drop a heavy on Jowan. He most probably can take its weight. Guess I'll find out if he can't.

'Jowan?'

'Hmm?'

'Do you ever wonder if it's all a fairy story after all?'

He checks my face. 'What? Church and stuff?'

'Yeah.'

He's quiet a moment and then comes out with this: 'Well, it *is* like a fairy story, isn't it?'

I look at him, shocked. 'What do you mean?' Surely he believes it all. I've counted on that or I wouldn't have asked.

'Well, you have God, the hero, riding into his own story. He has a quest—to win everyone back from the villain because he loves them and wants them to love him in return. And when he's paid the ransom, beaten the wicked villain, and broken the curse, the characters find out who they really are, and he tells them they're part of the King's family now and can share in everything he has. Well, then it all ends up as a sacred romance. Sounds like a Sleeping Beauty story to me.' He's laughing. 'A true one though. One big enough to live in.'

Has Jowan cracked his lid? Dad makes Christianity sound serious, not a romance. 'What about the commandments and doing unto others as we want them to do to us?'

Jowan shrugs. 'How I see it—what God wants is our hearts. We only have to think about him. The other stuff falls into place.'

'So, what do you think about?' I can't believe I'm asking a guy this, especially one that's not my boyfriend.

He stops walking. 'If I'm honest, I don't think about God a lot. There's Elaine, our music and a few other things.' He glances at me as he says this, as if he will explain what they are but he doesn't. He goes on, 'But I hope if it came to a crunch, God would come first.' It makes me wonder. Does God come first for me? Over Ryan? 'I don't think we really know who we are until we know what God thinks of us.'

'So, what would He think of me?' I don't expect Jowan to know how to answer. I've sung songs about Jesus loving me, but Jowan doesn't know how I've been thinking lately, or some of the movies I've sat through because I was too scared to make a scene.

Jowan keeps it light. 'He thinks you're just right, Essie. What do you expect?' He says 'just right' as though it has a deeper meaning, like fully loved and accepted. Maybe he's correct but I'm the one who doesn't feel I'm worthy.

Before I go to sleep I write Dad another email, even though I know he's in the house.

Hey, Dad, I miss you. I miss the way we used to do things and you were here all the time. Please don't forget us. I love you. Es. XXX

I read it over. It sounds like a note you write to someone who's died and put it on the coffin with the flowers. My finger hovers over the send button. Should I send it? My finger presses down. Sent.

I forgot to ask if he has a new phone. Why hasn't he told me? I don't want to upset Mum by asking. Maybe she doesn't know about it either.

16

As I anticipated, I haven't been able to get out of the soirée at the music school. Mrs Mangledorf assures me the piano in the RSL Hall has been better tuned this time. Last year it sounded like a catfight, and middle C wouldn't even work. That's tricky in a piece written in C major. Every time I had a double octave run I was in a battle to outdo the piano. Even Mrs M was wincing aloud. Usually, she tries to hide all her facial expressions in front of the parents.

I suggest to Mum that we walk in at halftime. They don't put the older ones on till later. You should see the look on her face. 'How would you feel if everyone stayed out when it was your turn?'

It's not a bad idea but I don't think Mum would understand. I give my Sigh of Resignation. Dad reckons I'm full of sighs and shut doors lately, but he doesn't do anything about it. Why doesn't he talk to Merryn and me more? Come home earlier? Answer my emails? He's not even coming to the soirée. He should be so lucky, but *I* have to go. Hello? A bit of fatherly support here would be helpful.

When we arrive, we are given a programme, and we find a

seat. They're wooden and in rows, real back-breakers. Mum tells me again how she used to go to the pictures here when she was my age. 'They put up a screen and had the projector just about there.'

She points back down the aisle. I don't even need to look. I can see how stories get passed down the ages so they can never be forgotten. I suppose if this place is still standing and I'm around here when I've got kids I'll be saying, like I'm programmed, 'Your grandmother used to come here to see movies. The projector was just about there.' I'm going to make sure I notice when my kids are bored. No one else in my house seems to know the meaning of the word.

This little kid climbs up onto the stage—he's no bigger than Tad. He plays 'Hickory Dickory Dock' on the piano. My body relaxes. The piano sounds okay at least, even if the kid does make it sound like the cat is coming down the clock and not the mouse. I glance at the programme. Oh no, it has *four pages*. Mum takes it off me since she keeps all the programmes in a memorabilia folder in the filing cabinet.

Mum sits through everything with a smile on her face. 'I remember when you played that one,' she says at least five times.

We have to go through all of this for Merryn's concert at the end of term as well. This year, since she's been involved in the Maypole dancing to be performed at the Cornish Festival in May, the school will put on a display for the parents. She'll be wearing my 19th century dress and apron. I miss Maypole dancing, especially now that I'm not doing it in high school.

Merryn's humming to herself, watching everything. Ten— how I wish I was still ten. Though Ryan wouldn't have kissed me if I was ten. Thinking about Ryan gets me through the next hour, and all of a sudden, it seems, it's my turn. I take my music onto the stage. Mrs M gives me a wary smile. I know she's got one eye on my nails. I've cut a few, the ones that have the most work in this piece.

Mrs M introduces me, and I start Mozart's 'Alla Turca'. After the first few bars I'm okay. This is one piece I know I can do passably well. It's just not music that everyone—except adults—raves about. When I finish, Mrs M smiles like an actor as the clapping starts and I bow, but I recognise the expression in her eyes; she's thinking I could have done it even better with no nails at all.

When I get back to my seat, Mum gives my arm a squeeze, as though I've just won a music scholarship, and the next person is already on the stage. It's the last act. The teachers usually leave a competent person for the finale. It makes all the parents think happily that's what their kid will be like if they leave them in the music school. I look up with interest and my breath dies in my throat.

It's Mary. Why did they leave her for last? I presumed she hadn't sung tonight because she wouldn't be ready after all, and then they put her on last? Her teacher is playing this flowing introduction on the piano. It sounds like the beginning of a romantic movie. Mary's standing there, waiting for her cue. She looks kind of hopeful. That's the word for it, I think. I slip down in my seat, not daring to watch. She'll be so embarrassed afterwards. How could her teacher be so mean?

Then she starts. *You are my hiding place* ... I gradually look up ... *a shelter from the storm.* I can't believe it. It's the same voice. The one I heard in the music school, the one powerful enough to penetrate the wall. I thought it must have been the teacher. Even Mary's first note is strong and the rest is incredible. Everyone is riveted. She's smiling as she sings, she knows she has us all in the hollow of her hand. Mary playing a crowd? Who would have thought? Even the little kids have stopped shuffling in their seats.

When she stops there's a second when I wipe my eyes and then all the parents are on their feet yelling 'Encore' like in old movies. Nothing like it has ever happened in the music school before. Some fathers are stamping on the floor—it sounds like a giant drum roll. Mary has to sing the chorus again while her teacher looks as if she's found the next winner of *The Voice*.

On the way out, just before we pass each other, everyone's congratulating Mary. When she's close enough, I smile and say, 'You were great.' I'm embarrassed that I didn't think she could sing so well but at least she doesn't know that. Mary gives me her little smile. It's still the same smile. She's just wowed the whole music school audience and she still looks as if she's on the verge of learning something new.

On the way home Merryn can't stop talking about it which means Mary made a huge impression. 'She made me think things, Essie. Like I was on a horse, galloping along the beach. It was like a movie and I was the star.'

Guess it is a first for Merryn and me. Let's face it, kids playing 'Hickory Dickory Dock' aren't going to fire your imagination.

'Did she do that to you too, Essie?'

I just nod. I don't say how I felt like I was flying, a travelling spirit, at last, rising over the heroes' hall, the clouds firm under me like the sea when I'm swimming. Merryn seems content at last and this is when I first get the idea about Mary.

17

It's the next Monday and Chloe and Ashleigh are busy on the Lunch Bench discussing what outfits they'll buy in the city. Ashleigh's stepfather is taking them down on the weekend. Mum says: what we can't buy here, we don't need. She believes in supporting local business. The girls are still discussing The Club. I was hoping they'd forget that, and I go off to find Mary. The library's a likely place since sports practise is over. First, I see Beth, researching for an assignment.

'Hey,' I say.

She grins and makes space for me at the table. 'Whatcha been doing?'

'Music, homework, you know?'

'Yeah.'

'You?'

She looks at me before she answers. 'Saw Marty down the street on the weekend.'

'He talk to you?'

'Yeah, he's pretty busy though ...' Her voice fades away and I know what she feels.

'I bet he likes you though.'

'You reckon?' She flushes and I grin at her.

'Have to go. See you around?'

'Sure.'

When I find Mary behind the history stacks, she's talking to Laila. I'd thought girls with headscarves would be shy and demure, the sort who do everything Daddy says. But Laila's not like that at all.

Mary's still nice to me, even though I don't deserve it. She's got that cute smile of hers on. Laila's just told a joke by the look of them, faces pink, shoulders shaking. It pulls me up short. Laila has what Mum would call a bright personality; would they want me barging in? Maybe now isn't the right time to ask Mary if she'd sing with our band. But I do it.

'Um, Mary. I was just wondering if you'd like to sing in a talent quest. That is, Jowan in our class and I and a few other guys have started a band, and I think you'd be perfect for it.' Imagine if Chloe heard me. Mary perfect for something? But she is. She has the most perfect voice.

Mary is staring at me, not saying a word. Laila has nothing to say either, but she looks at Mary to see what she'll do. It makes me wonder if Mary has confided in Laila about me, and instantly I back away. 'Well, you think about it. I'll be around.'

I just hope Mary picks the right moment when she gives me her answer. In front of Chloe just before afternoon class would not be good. Chloe would freeze me out again, or at the very least, not let me concentrate on my maths with notes asking 'What was that? A band?' And what if Laila comes too? But Laila looks okay to me and I find myself thinking about her during maths. She's clever enough to help with algebra. As I remember she is also a lot of fun.

Mary sees me in the toilets after school. 'Where does the

band play?' she asks. I tell her about The Café down Jetty Road. 'Cool,' she says. I tell her when the next practice will be. 'So, do you want to have lunch with Laila and me tomorrow and you can tell me about it?'

I stare at her. She's being kind, but doesn't she know anything? Chloe will wipe me if I have lunch with Mary, and especially Laila. I'll never get a date with Ryan, an eventuality that I hope is close. Chloe keeps hinting even though Ashleigh still hardly mentions him. 'I'll see,' I say. Mary doesn't look disappointed, but she turns to dry her hands.

All the way home I have the weird feeling I'm missing something. There's such a heavy stone in the pit of my stomach. When I take the dogs down to the beach I think about it some more. Why are things so complicated? Why can't everybody like each other? Then it wouldn't matter who you spent time with. Your friends would be happy for you whatever you did then. I'm sick of all Chloe's rules. And yet when I with her and she's being nice I feel good, it's afterwards that I feel confused, when I think of things she's said that don't add up. Maybe I could get to know Ryan better by myself—just walk up to him and start talking. Who am I kidding? The only guy I can do that with is Jowan.

I wade through the sand, and the sea comes into view. There's a windsurfer with a see-through sail, like a giant dragonfly cutting across the waves. Then I see Jowan playing water volleyball with the kids. Merryn is there too. Rebecca must have invited her. I say 'Hi' to my little sister and she smiles quietly back but I can see the shine in her eyes. She wants me to join in. I look up the beach. It's far too early for Ryan to be training, so I throw myself into the game. So do the dogs.

'Hey,' Jowan says. 'How about we choose teams?'

I take Merryn and Rebecca. Jowan is left with Desi, Luke

and Tad. None of them wants to play on a girls' side anyway. Tyler and Vinny play on both teams, or is it their own? Once Vinny has that ball, it's like wrenching a clam open to get it out of his mouth.

'If it was pumped up more, he wouldn't be able to get his mouth around it,' I say, tugging on Vinny's jaw.

Vinny growls for fun and Tyler actually prances around us. Then Jowan helps me from the other side of Vinny. We both pull but Tyler jumps on us as well and Jowan and I collapse on the sand, the ball beneath us, laughing so hard there's hardly a noise. Tyler and Vinny stand with quivering legs apart, ready to pounce.

Then I remember where we are, and I stand up, brushing the sand off my legs. 'I'd better take them for a run now,' I say. Rebecca and Merryn groan.

'But it's so much fun,' Merryn whines. 'You're different now, you don't want to do things with me.' Don't I bring her to the beach now? But I still feel guilty.

'We'll do it another time.' I sound just like Mum when I say that. Is Merryn comparing me to Jowan or what?

Jowan's watching me. 'Great to see you have fun, Essie.' He grins like Vinny and it makes me bristle. What does he mean? I know how to have fun.

I jog up the beach with the boys crisscrossing the sand in front of me. If I run two kilometres, they must run ten, sniffing every suspicious little mound and footprint.

Ryan doesn't show and I decide I will have to take decisive action where he is concerned. I may have to get serious about Chloe's clubbing idea. If a boy is worth having, is any sacrifice too much? Look what Benedick was prepared to do for Beatrice.

Later, there's an email from Dad.

Hi Es, I'm so sorry I can't spend more time at home right now. I'm doing the work of two people I reckon. I had no idea when I took it on, but don't worry it won't be forever. Always know I love you and I know it's no excuse to say I'm working more for you and Merryn. I can see that neither of you are happy about it. Nor am I happy that I have a digital relationship with you when we sleep in the same house.

Tell me what you wrote in those texts I didn't get. Keep your focus on the Lord, sweetheart. Love Dad.

I know Dad doesn't lie, but I'm confused. His email sounds so good and it makes sense. But what about that woman who has his phone? That's what she said: *This is my phone.*

18

Chloe asks me on Wednesday if I'm coming to The Club with them for sure. 'Are you up to it?' she asks. 'Ryan's already said he's coming.'

It's like she's dangling Ryan on a string and just like a puppet I don't hesitate. 'Of course.'

I see the little look of satisfaction come over Chloe's face and I presume it means I've passed a test. Maybe they think I'm mature enough now to go out with them. Though I don't want to end up doing anything that's bad for me—the porn movie can still give me a creepy dream. Surely, I can *pretend* I'm drinking? All that matters is that Ryan will be there. He'll look after me, and make sure none of those horrible things that Mum says happen in nightclubs happens to me—like spiked drinks and people dying from Ice. But I don't dwell on it too much, not even about how I can't look remotely eighteen as Ashleigh does, even in school uniform. She's so confident and beautiful she could pass as the Cornish Festival Fairy Queen.

Chloe says she'll handle everything. All I can think of is Ryan kissing me, which I have now remembered as more romantic than I thought at the time. I realise it must have been the shock.

Erik picks us up after school and I go to Chloe's place for a practice run on looking eighteen. She has a few extra outfits for me to try on, none of which I'd be able to leave my house in. Chloe understands. 'You should stay with me that night. Ashleigh might too. We can get ready together. I'll do your makeup.' She's scrutinising my face as though it will be a difficult job and she's working out which way will be easier.

'What about ID?' I ask.

'Derek will handle that.' Chloe gives a private smile. There are still a lot of things she doesn't share with me. Things Ashleigh and she talk about when I'm not there. I probably wouldn't want to know, but I can't help that little niggle of doubt about not being good enough to be confided in.

Putting on makeup takes ages. 'This is the latest lengthening mascara,' Chloe says, holding it ready to brush my eyelashes. She has a palette of 150 shades of eye shadow too. 'Let's try this colour brown—it will highlight your eyes.' She applies it with feathery touches while I feel grateful she's saying nice things to me again.

I glance at my phone and see the time. 'On no! I'm so sorry I have to go.' I snatch the facial wipes. 'I have to run.'

Chloe's put out. 'What's so important? You haven't tried the lipsticks yet.' I'm torn, especially as her frown is growing deeper and darker.

'I know you've really put yourself out for me today and used all your special make-up to try on me—' How can I explain to soften the blow? She spends all this time with me so why do I feel like I'm her project. And I could lose my ticket to The Club just like that, but Merryn will be home alone too long. No use trying to explain that to Chloe. She has no younger siblings. She doesn't have to think about anything except what she wants to do next.

'I'm sorry, Chloe—family responsibilities.' I can't mention Dad. I'm sure she thinks he's dead, but Dad is foremost in my mind. If he should come home early—not that he does lately—but if he should and find Merryn alone, my life won't be worth living. I make a quick exit and jog as far as I can with my bag jiggling on my back, but I end up doing a power walk, my lungs burning.

When I reach the back gate, there are no dogs to greet me. That's odd. 'Merryn?' No answer. I race inside, the door's unlocked. Her bag is there, but no Merryn. Where would she go? And with the dogs? I drop my bag and head for the beach. Merryn is no match for Tyler and Vinny when they smell the sea after being in the yard all day.

I must be losing 500 calories but even this heartening thought can't erase the fear. I'd be devastated if something happened to Merryn. She's my little sister. She's adorable and I've been so selfish, just thinking about my own problems. Here's me thinking Dad hasn't spent enough time with us, but I've been just the same. She's right, I haven't done enough things with her. I should have been doing more, with Dad so busy and Mum working, not less.

When I first get down to the water, I can't see her anywhere. No excited dog barks. This is a quiet country beach but predators could still visit. I check our jetty. Underneath and around the corner. The rocks. No Merryn. I trip over a rock and tie my shoelaces up again. Which way would she go? North. I head up that way but the sand is pristine. I run back to where I started and head further down the beach towards the town and the next jetty. If she's taken the dogs with her she must have entered the beach further up. That would mean more time on the road. What if she was picked up before she even got to the beach.

Jesus, help me find her. I shouldn't have been late. *I'm so sorry.*

It's not until I pass the shelter shed that I see paw prints. Plenty of them. It's like seeing double, it could be Tyler and Vinny, crisscrossing as they usually do, a small human footprint held in the middle. There are a lot of other footprints too, but I hope I'm tracking the right ones. The footprints lead to the next jetty. There are a lot of holes down that way. She wouldn't go in the water by herself, surely? I start to jog again, but I'm running low on energy, my calf muscles kill and I have such a stitch. All I can hear in my head is Merryn saying I don't do enough with her. Her crying over her sums. How could I be so mean? Merryn is more important to me than anyone. She's my baby sister.

Then I see the dogs. They're bouncing in the water as usual, spray enveloping them. Can't spot Merryn. Tyler's barking. Something must be wrong. I run harder. I'm so puffed and my throat full of tears I can't yell out. Vinny sees me first. He gives a bark and rushes up to me, his tail swinging.

'Where's Merryn, boy?' He bounds back to the sea after I pat him, and I see why. Jowan emerges from the water, spray flying, the kids with him, including Merryn. Jowan has a ball. Vinny races into the fray. I don't act as relieved as I feel. The fear has morphed into a dark storm. All that pent-up emotion wondering what could have happened to Merryn spills out and it's not pretty. I stride over.

'Merryn! Why did you leave the house?' I'm shouting and I can't stop myself. 'It was unlocked! Anyone could have broken in.' It's not what I want to say: *Hey, I'm sorry I was late. I thought something horrible had happened to you. Life wouldn't be the same ...*

Merryn stares at me, her mouth open, then she gulps. 'Jowan came and you weren't there. I didn't think it would matter.' She suddenly remembers she isn't the only one at fault. 'You were late.'

'You should've left a note.' I'm practically crying, trembling all over, and I ball up my fists trying to control myself. I never lose my cool like this. What's happening to me? It's like everything since the beginning of term is pressing on my chest. My breathing is ragged as I move from foot to foot. All the kids are standing in a semi-circle staring at me. I flop on the ground with my head in my hands.

Jowan walks over. I think he's going to put a hand on my shoulder. If he does I'll throw it off. But he doesn't touch me. His voice does though. It's warm and calm. 'It's okay now, Essie. I'm sorry, I should have thought about that when I picked her up.'

I feel the relief soothing the fear and I try to let it out in even breaths, even if they're still hot with steam.

'We saw dolphins.' Merryn's watching me. I stand up and I'm sad that she's so wary of me. I manage a smile. I've neglected her. I should know how that feels.

'Do you want to come with me now, Merryn? We can get an ice-cream.' Her eyes widen. She even forgets the game, yells back a quick 'Bye' to Rebecca, and slips her hand in mine. It's so small, reminding me how vulnerable she is and so trusting.

'You were worried, weren't you?' She looks across at me as I bend to pick up the dogs' leads.

I give her a shaky grin. 'Yeah. Hope I never have to go through that again.' That's what mothers feel like. No wonder it took Mum ten years before she'd let me take Merryn down to the beach by myself.

Merryn's choosing her ice-cream already. 'We aren't there yet,' I say.

'It pays to be ready.' She sounds older than ten and I look at her again. Mum said one day Merryn and I will be good friends. Maybe she's right.

On Jetty Road, we tie the dogs to a veranda post and passers-by 'ooh' and 'aah' over them while we choose ice-cream. Well, *I* choose and Merryn copies me—low-fat English Toffee. Wouldn't she have liked a rainbow one or one with M & Ms?

We eat the ice-creams on our jetty. I'm thinking about that time Jowan and I ate ice-cream here when Merryn asks me this question. 'Do you think I'm fat, Essie?'

I'm shocked. She's never said anything like this before. 'Fat? You? Who told you that?'

'No one has to tell me things.' She looks miffed, but I know some kid has said it to her. 'I want to look like you, Essie. You're so cool. Everyone says so.'

'Merryn—' I squint at her against the setting sun. She's not skinny but nor is she fat. And she shouldn't be thinking about that at ten. A tide of feeling rushes up into my chest and I recognise it: I want to protect Merryn. Who could have said such a rotten thing to spoil her joy in life, her innocence? 'Merryn, you mustn't take any notice if anyone picks on the way you look. That's terribly wrong of them. And you're really cute.' Listen to me, but it's different for me of course because I'm fifteen. I have to be concerned about certain things. I swear Merryn can read my mind.

'You stand in front of the mirror and check you look alright. All the time. I want to be just like you.'

'That's different. I'm fifteen.'

She doesn't believe me. *Oh Essie, what have you done?*

19

When we arrive home, Dad's sitting in the lounge. This is a first. I've been waiting for him to come home early for so long I don't know what to feel. I should be excited. We could go to the jetty.

'You're home,' is all I say. It sounds catty.

He smiles at Merryn and asks how his little Merrie is, but she ignores him. Lately, she's grown out of Merrie and he doesn't even know. He raises his eyebrows at me. It's hard to smile. I feel so bad not being home in time for Merryn.

'How come the house was left open, hmm?' His 'hmm's' aren't as innocent as they sound. They are bridging notes between one chord and the next, usually from soft to loud.

Merryn decides to be ten again and climbs up on his knee. I'd like to do that too. I could tell him about Ryan and how I'm not quite the sort of girl he asks out. I could tell him about Chloe and how hard it is to be her friend, to not make mistakes. But I doubt he'd understand. He doesn't know what it's like at school. I bet when he was young, it was simple. His family didn't have a TV for a start. It was church that guided people in what to do and I bet they never mentioned the things we have to think about today. Now we know how we are supposed to look, to act. We hear about it all the time from the media. It's a hard road to travel.

'I came home early,' Merryn says, 'and went to the beach with the Tallacks. I left the house open. Essie came and found me. I'm sorry, Dad.'

Dad looks at me. 'And you were too worried to know what you were doing, I suppose?' He isn't cross. Amazing. Merryn has totally diffused what could have been a crescendo. All she did was tell the simple truth. 'Next time lock the house, okay?' We both nod as Merryn slips off Dad's knee to get a snack. I head for my room but Dad calls me.

'I need to discuss something with you.' Uh oh. 'Your nails.' Just like Dad to finally be home and instead of doing something together, he gets involved in trivial stuff. I stiffen. My nails are my own business, doesn't he know that? Mum does surely. Why would she tell him? I hide them behind my back.

'Everyone's growing their nails at school,' I say. It sounds lame. Dad's still not cross, more amused.

'Chloe and her cronies, no doubt?' Then his face changes. I'm in defence mode, sword and shield ready. I'm about to shout—I can feel it bubbling up inside me—how he's never home and now he is and he's criticising my nails?

But the look on his face disarms me. It's switched to his worried frown. 'Essie, I hope you don't take too much notice of what other people say. You know what you believe, so you know who you are.' I do? I wish he'd help me remember. He must see the uncertainty in my face for he adds, 'When you know God loves you totally, you don't have to live in anyone else's story. Write your own script, Es. Stand tall.'

This is so unexpected, I'm wordless. I was prepared to fight for my nails, but I don't know what to say to this.

'Okay, Es?' I think I've just been given a profound 'Dad moment'. I can only nod at him with my lip screwed up, and I escape to my bedroom where I've moved my piano to play some jazz music we've picked out for the band.

Since it's Thursday night, it's my shift to help in Aunty Joy's gift shop. Mum drives me down. She doesn't say much, but she mentions Dad's little pep talk. 'Dad said something to you about your nails, I hear.' I don't answer. I'm not too pleased with her since she must have told him. Who's ever heard of fathers noticing their daughter's nails, unless they're painted bright red? And mine aren't. They're getting nice and square on the end. I'm thinking of getting false ones glued on like Ashleigh's. Those false ones even look strong enough to hold down a piano key.

'Eseld, when are you going to cut them? Mrs Mangledorf even rang about it. She spoke to your father—she has high hopes for you. She says you have real talent in piano, gifted even.'

'Gifted! Me?' I laugh.

Mum nods at the road ahead. 'That's what she said. Of course, everyone's gifted in their own way, but she thinks you're really good, Eseld, and your nails are holding you back.'

'But I don't want to be a concert pianist!' I don't mean it to come out as a shout, but it does. Mum looks across at me quickly with a worried look. She's getting those a lot lately. 'I just want to have fun. I don't like her music anymore either.'

'Her music, as you put it, is a program, so you can learn the piano properly.' Mum says this in her patient explaining voice, but I can detect the near hysteria she's trying hard to control.

'Why can't she use interesting music, like the jazz stuff we've picked out for the band?'

'The band is a good interest for you, Eseld—it's an extra—'

111

'So I don't get bored with the real music, right?' My tone is rising again, and Mum crunches the gears.

'Damn.'

'Mum, your halo is slipping.' She doesn't look too happy, but she drops the subject of the nails at least.

The truth is my halo is slipping too. When have I spoken to her like this? And she's not even telling me off. When I was Merryn's age, if Mum told me to cut my nails, I would have done it straight away. Actually, I can remember her cutting them for me. Bet she wishes she could do that now.

Aunty Joy is more fun than a parent. She can look at my nails and admire them and not worry about the money she's wasting on music lessons. She can treat me like a real person. Parents can't always do that because they are concerned about the responsibility they have, and probably what other parents will say about them if their daughter gives up her piano lessons.

'What's with the nails?' Aunty Joy says. I'm not surprised. You expect aunts to notice your nails and I stretch them out for her to see. I can tell she wishes she has some the same, but she says, 'Be hard to play the piano with those, I suppose.'

I fold them up again. When aunts are your mother's younger sister they throw in some support for your parent, so I try not to take it personally. It doesn't work. Right now everything is annoying me: the music, Mum, Dad talking about my nails. And that's not even mentioning Chloe. I feel like an acrobat losing my balance on the wire and there's no safety net.

After my homework, I sit on the bed and think. My mind is whirring with white noise. Chloe's in my head shouting I'm not a good friend, Ryan's smiling, leaning closer, Jowan's calling me a swan, Dad's saying to live my own story, and I'm shouting at

Mum. I close my eyes to try concentrating on one thing—Mum. It's too late to talk. She'll be in bed, so I send a text.

I'm sorry, lots happening. Love you.

I feel so strung out. I wish I could relax. Should I send a text to Chloe? To say sorry for leaving her house early? But I don't feel like it. What if she's in a bad mood and goes for me? She can see things that I've never even done.

I design an invite for dad: *You are invited on a date to have ice-cream on the jetty.* I draw the jetty with two stick figures sitting at the end, with a pelican on the lamp post. How long since we've done that?

Hey Dad

In those texts I wrote about having an ice-cream on the jetty together. Remember the jetty? How we used to go there? It was our special place at the end where we could imagine we were out at sea. Remember the sealion pup that looked in trouble? The hungry pelican? Those dolphins that jumped in front of us and splashed us. They knew we were watching them. Maybe that was years ago, but I'd love to still do that with you even though I'm fifteen.

Love you, Essie.

I attach the invite. What good will it do? I'm sobbing when I get into bed and I pull the quilt over my head.

20

It's Friday night and I've managed to get to the band practice at The Café. It's been complicated because Chloe wanted me to go home with her to try on more outfits for The Club excursion—which is how I'm thinking of it—since it will be the time when I learn lots. And Ryan will see how mature I can look.

Jowan says we need to have the band practices on Friday nights now to suit Kris and Marty since they're in Year 12. Beth will be interested in these practices as well since she likes Marty. Youth group is where we mostly catch up. Mary is cool with Friday nights. So is Jowan because the youth group is afterwards so he says it works fine for everyone. I can't very well say I need to go to a clubbing practice. I hope Chloe doesn't decide to do the trip to The Club on a Friday night. Then I'll be really stuffed.

I introduce Mary to the guys. Laila comes too with her older brother. He's called Habib and has laughing eyes. The music starts and it's more exciting than Mrs Mangledorf's lessons. We jam awhile first to warm up. Laila and her brother clap. He's got the same style of personality as she does. They should give him a box drum, I bet he'd have good rhythm. We play the music Jowan's picked out as well. We do okay. The guys are great on their guitars. Kris's bass is so good we don't need drums, and Marty picks Blues rhythms like a pro. And Jowan's sax is cool. When I'm playing, I shut my eyes on the parts I know well and imagine I'm on the beach at sunset. The sax gives a true jazz feel to the band, and I'm learning heaps about improvisation, something you don't get taught in classical piano. Kris is giving me all these tips since he plays keyboard too. He's even good at back-up vocals. The flag on the castle, though, is Mary. When she starts singing the first time all the guys lose their rhythm. If we do well in this quest, it will be because of Mary. Even Laila hasn't heard Mary sing before. She's standing there, both hands on her cheeks.

'You are very talented, Mary,' Laila says when we stop for a break. Mary smiles that little smile.

Mary has to be the humblest person I know, and I discover another talent of hers. She has a great sense of humour. You'd never know at school. All the guys in the band love her. She has them in stitches. She knows a lot about music and that's what her jokes are about. Chloe would be shocked. She wouldn't think Mary is socially apt enough to make people laugh. I wish I could tell her she's wrong. It would be pointless, as Chloe believes she is always right and nothing I can say can shift her. It feels bad thinking of her like this, but I'm starting to see more clearly. When I'm with her I can't seem to though. Mary, Laila, Beth—none of them make me feel anxious like Chloe does. Even when she's being nice now, I'm waiting for the barb.

Mary, Laila and I order ice coffees and the guys get chocolate malted milkshakes. Laila's wearing her scarf and we're all getting along so well I ask her about it. She seems wary and I say, 'You don't need to answer if you don't want to, but do *you* choose to wear the scarf?'

'Yes.' She says it simply. 'It makes me feel more—' she's searching for the right word '—pure.'

I sit back. Would I feel purer in a scarf? 'I don't think I could wear something that says so openly what I am.' Or is it because I'm not so sure who or what I am? I admire Laila's confidence.

She shrugs. 'So, it *is* what I am. At least if everyone knows then they don't have to guess.'

'Do people say things? Kids tease you?'

She half grins. 'I've been called a terrorist.' Mary and I don't smile. We know Laila is not amused. 'But at least I know who my real friends are.'

That sounds fine but her scarf is a red rag to some people. A target to aim at. I saw this YouTube video about the Egyptian girls who are Christian and have a cross tattooed on the back of their hand. A girl was raped because of that cross. It was skinned off her hand too. How depraved is that?

'I think most people at school are used to my hijab,' Laila says.

'Yes,' Mary joins in. 'People in our classes don't notice it anymore.'

It's funny, Laila believes different things from me but it's easier talking to her than to Chloe and Ashleigh who say they don't believe anything. Mary too, she mightn't believe either, but she lets Laila and me be ourselves. It's made me think. Maybe I don't need to wear a headscarf or a tattoo to show who I am, but at least Laila's not afraid to.

The wind is high as Jowan and I leave The Café. Waves are washing up the jetty pylons. We haven't had a storm for ages. Some people are frightened by lightning and thunder and whether the sea will swallow houses on the beachfront, but I'm not. I love the way the sky bursts into forked silver flames. The crash soon after is like a concert bass drum. Music with a light show, what a combination. We get wet because Jowan stops still, hugging his sax case, and lifts his face to the sky. 'I love rain,' he shouts. We laugh as we run to the Tallack's car.

At home, after I dry off, I check my emails. Dad's answered. He can't do the date for a while yet, something's coming up at work. But he'll get back to me.

I answer: *Cool, Dad. Can't wait to spend some time with you. Sorry you have to work so hard. I hardly see you. So much to tell you.*

My eyes blink as I stop typing. I've just realised: I have a digital relationship with my dad and all I want is a hug.

21

Mum's taken Merryn down the street to the dentist. Looks like Merryn is going to need braces. She's a bit young yet but Mum's getting a second opinion. I'll cheer up Merryn when she gets back, but right now I'm taking the dogs down to the beach for their daily constitutional. The sky's still overcast from the storm but at least it's not raining. When we cross the bitumen and reach the grass, Vinny starts to pull at the lead. 'Hang on, boy.' Once we reach the sand, I unhook them. So glad we don't have to keep dogs on leads like on city beaches. How would they run properly? They'd trip me up with all their sniffing and investigating. Tyler and Vinny would make great detective dogs.

They run past a couple entwined on one towel. Tyler goes back for a sniff and I call him. 'C'mon, boy.' I start jogging so he'll chase me. That couple wouldn't be pleased with him. Mum would be shocked and tell me to avert my eyes and walk briskly past. I wonder what the big deal about making out is anyway. In every story or movie—except my folktale novels—the characters jump into bed. It's normal for the twenty-first century. You're considered weird now if you don't. Dad's still back in the nineteenth century. There's nothing wrong with saying 'No', he says. We even hear about sex as a subject at school. They must think we're all doing it because they tell us everything we need to know, except that religions agree with Dad and Mum.

I couldn't tell Ashleigh about abstinence. She thinks abstinence is when you refrain from eating foods that are bad for your body. I'm not silly, I know not *every*one has sex. Laila wouldn't, for instance. Her big brother would be with her wherever she went. When would she ever be alone with a guy? She wouldn't even have been kissed. But I have, oh Ryan. I wonder what being with him totally would be like? He'd be loving: *I've been longing to do this just with you, Essie. You are so beautiful, I can't live without you.* Then I remember the movie night at Chloe's. Will I ever get those images out of my mind? I hope nothing like that happens to me.

At The Club I'm sure I'll find out what Ryan thinks about me. That little excursion won't be for a while yet. Apparently, Derek's having some trouble with our ID cards. Chloe will tell me when.

This is when I see the mounds of ladybirds. I don't know what they are at first and then I realise, they are *dead* ladybirds. Thousands of them. Like they'd been washed up by the sea. How could something like that happen? They belong on the land. We need ladybirds. Tears prick the top of my nose. The shock of thousands of dead ladybirds makes me feel so sad, as if the worry of Dad and Chloe, even Ryan, has hit again and the tears flow. I stroll up the beach. More and more little mounds of dead ladybirds. They're uncountable. The boys sniff them and bound on. I kneel to watch the ladybirds as if I'm mourning at a grave. And then I see movement. They are not all dead. One here, one there staggers out of the pile. I run to the next pile. There are a few survivors. I feel weirdly relieved, like the world is turning the right side up again. But how did a whole population of ladybirds drown?

In the middle of this reverie, I feel the sand shaking under my feet. It's rhythmic, like a bass drum. For a moment I think it's Ryan, jogging, but it's too heavy. Hoofbeats, it has to be. I turn and my jaw drops as I focus. A white horse streams towards me, spray flying up from her hooves. But of course, it's Jowan. He looks like he's ridden down from a station up north. He pulls Elaine in beside me. His grin is wide and infectious. Elaine nods her head and her mane dances around her face. She is beautiful.

'Wanna ride?'

I wipe my eyes with the back of my hand and Jowan's smile falls. 'You okay?' I point to the mounds of ladybirds, and he frowns.

'Dead ladybirds,' I say. 'Do you know why?' He shakes his head.

Then he smiles. 'Ride with me. It'll make you feel better.'

The boys have bounded over to check out Elaine. Vinny's keeping his distance, but I have to call Tyler away from Elaine's back hooves.

'Don't worry, she's used to dogs,' Jowan says. Then he leans down to me. 'C'mon, they'll keep up.' He reaches out his arm. 'Put your foot on mine and jump.' I take his hand and he pulls me up. He's surprisingly strong. I land on Elaine's back behind him. There's no saddle so I guess I'll have to hold onto Jowan. He takes off his helmet and hands it to me, looking apologetic. 'We didn't always wear helmets back home—town rules, I'm afraid.' I manage to get the strap done up in time.

'Don't go too fast,' I say, but he doesn't hear me for he's urged Elaine forward. I don't think we're galloping, maybe cantering. At first, I bump Elaine's back every time it rises up to meet me, but I catch on to how Jowan's moving up and down and I move with him. It's the most incredible feeling. This must be what pure joy is. It's even overcome my gloom over the ladybirds. Elaine slows to a trot. That rhythm is more difficult, but I think of it as a song we're playing together. I glance back at the dogs. Their mouths are wide, panting, but they're having fun too. Jowan's taller than me so I can't see over his shoulder, but it doesn't matter. The sea twinkles at me from the side, quiet again after the storm.

Jowan half turns. 'You okay?' I just grin and nod. His eyes are bright, and he clicks to Elaine, pushes his heels into her sides and she canters again. Then she gallops. I hold Jowan tighter. I've got both hands clenched onto my wrists around his middle. I've never had such a mixture of feelings—no make-believe ride at the show will ever compare. This is for real.

Then we slow, and Jowan turns Elaine's head. 'We'd better pick up the dogs,' he says. I laugh. We'd left them behind, but their tails start wagging when they see us returning.

'Elaine needed a good run,' Jowan says.

'So what's her stable like?'

'Great. It's not far. Farms just seem to roll down to the beach here.' He sounds amazed and I've never thought of that as special before, but I can see now it is. 'The farm's got baby animals—a tourist thing probably.'

'I've heard about that but never been.' Bet Merryn would like that.

'But I have to exercise Elaine.' By Jowan's tone, I can tell it will be the favourite time of his day.

'A white horse is amazing,' I say.

'She's not a true white, she's really a grey. See her muzzle? Her skin is dark underneath her hair. And her eyes are dark.'

'She's gorgeous.'

We walk back to our jetty, the boys panting beside us. Our

beach is one of the few in the state that cars can still drive on. Looks like that includes horses.

Getting off is awkward. Jowan holds my arm to let me down but I still land in a heap on the sand with Vinny licking my face. Jowan's off Elaine and beside me before I can even say 'Ow'.

'You okay, Essie? I'm sorry—I shouldn't have taken you so far. Have you ever been riding?'

I shake my head, but I smile at him. 'It's okay—it was worth it.' I stand up and Jowan supports me. My legs are shaky, and they ache from being stretched across Elaine's back. My bum's a bit sore too, but I don't say so, just give it a surreptitious rub.

'Are you sure you're okay? I can't come and help you home. I have to take Elaine back to the stable.' He looks so concerned that I want to put him at ease.

'It's fine. I'll have to get better at it, won't I?'

He relaxes. 'Sure you will. So, you liked it then?'

'Yeah.' I don't say much, but I think he knows what I'm feeling. He swings up onto Elaine and I hand him the helmet. He has the reins in one hand as he clips the helmet strap. Elaine snorts and shakes her head. 'I'll bring two helmets next time, just in case.'

I watch him as they trot off, and I call the boys. How can they bounce around in the waves after running all that way? I put their leads on and we walk slowly home. I'll have to ask Jowan to give Merryn a turn. She'll think she's died and gone to paradise. Jowan truly has a gift—he can make me forget myself.

At home, I'm supposed to be doing homework but I Google drowned ladybirds instead. I discover that this one species gathers together after hibernation and often they get relocated by a sea breeze. Except, our sea breeze turned into a storm.

22

School's not going well today. This is becoming the refrain of a sad song. Chloe's been stuck into me like a ten-centimetre pin since the first lesson. 'So, you ride horses on the beach?' She sounds vicious, and dare I think it, jealous. I'm steeling myself for the cone of silence again.

'What do you mean?' How did she find out? Jowan would say our school is like a flock of galahs: no secrets. He wouldn't be wrong.

'You were seen. Fancy galloping past the Life Saving Club like that, holding onto some other guy? You've got a nerve, Essie Pederick.' Life Saving Club? How could I not have noticed? At least she doesn't know it was Jowan. All the same, this feeling of dread is uncurling in my gut. Ryan? Did he see? But I don't even need to ask.

'Ryan saw you.' So that's how Chloe knows. Ryan would have told Ashleigh.

'So what?' I say, hoping it sounds like it's no big deal. At first I think wow, he must like me, he even recognised me with a helmet on. But inside I'm shaking. Why this awful fear? Am I afraid of Chloe? Why? Because she could make me lose a chance with Ryan?

Chloe comes out with it. 'You're a two-timer.'

'No, I'm not.' Oh, the injustice. 'That guy—he's a friend.' I'd like to say 'brother', that's what it feels like, but Chloe already knows I don't have one.

'When girls like someone they don't hang onto other guys that tight.'

They do if they think they're going to fall off. I know defending myself to Chloe won't do any good. Once she thinks she knows the truth you can't shift her. But I defend myself anyway. 'It wasn't like that.'

'Try that one on Ryan,' Chloe says, smirking.

'What do you mean?'

She gives a superior lift of her eyebrows and glances at her nails. 'I'm not sure that Ryan will want you to come to The Club with us now.'

My poor insides are sinking to my knees. They've been all over the place this morning, but there's anger in there too, for I see something I haven't before. It's Chloe who doesn't want me to go. Has Ryan actually said that? Or is it Chloe trying to call the shots?

As it happens a miracle happens. All day I sweat it out. I don't see Ryan or his mates at school, and Chloe and Ashleigh don't invite me into their conversation on the Lunch Bench. They ignore me again as if I'm not there. It feels like a punishment. I don't know why I bother sitting there. Just letting them know I'm innocent, I guess.

When I get home my phone rings. It's Ryan.

'Hey, Essie.'

'Hey.' I wait for him to bring up the horse-riding incident, while I try to calm my thumping heart. It's galloping way too fast and it's not all from excitement.

'Just rang for a chat.' He talks about his swimming and training, the Life Saving Club. 'I'm training to compete in the Ironman Swim Competition next January. So I have to train a lot. Swimming as well as running. I'll be finished my life saving medal at the end of the year.'

This is interesting stuff—pity I can't relax enough to concentrate and enjoy it. I can't get a word in and he hasn't asked about me but maybe he's too nervous, like me. I'm still waiting for Ryan's 'but', when he mentions The Club. Here it comes.

'I'm looking forward to our little date,' he says.

That doesn't hit home straight away. I'm expecting him to say why it's off, but he doesn't. He sounds more interested in me than he has before. 'So let's do it soon, Essie?'

'Sure,' I say, wondering what part of the conversation I've missed. Maybe my conscious mind turned off for a few moments, so it didn't hear the hard part.

'Brett and Derek will come too, there'll be six of us, but I'm sure we'll find some time alone. Would you like that, Essie?'

'Mm-hmm, yes.' What a stupid question. Of course, I want to be alone with him. I'm wondering why he's asking, but then he finishes off the conversation.

'See you around, Essie. Cheers.'

'Cheers.' He never mentioned the horse riding, yet Chloe said he knows. I think about that for a while. Could it possibly mean I am more interesting because I've been seen with another guy? Ryan must think he has some competition. I grin. If only he knew. I could have told him and he wouldn't have to worry about it, but I didn't get a chance.

It's later than usual and I'm trying to write another email to Dad in bed before I go to sleep. How do I say I think I have a problem? I don't want a full-scale investigation into Chloe's and my relationship, goodness what would she do if she knew I was discussing her, but something isn't quite right. It's so much easier to talk to Beth or Mary and Laila, and I can see that. Why is it so hard with Chloe, even Ashleigh? I don't like to be out of sorts with anyone. But nor do I like being called out for something I'm not. Or is she right? If I was serious about Ryan, maybe I shouldn't be spending any time with Jowan.

Just then I hear Mum talking to Dad. When I'm in my room I can never hear their discussions. This is a first.

'It's like being married to a doctor or a teacher—they're either not home or they're marking at home.' Dad speaks but I can't understand him. He's probably too tired to raise his voice. 'Alby, the girls need you. I need you—' Their door shuts. Good old Mum.

I shut down my iPad and lay in bed halfway to sleep. Mum and Dad are so good at keeping their feelings hidden from us girls, but this is the first time Mum hasn't waited until the door was shut. Poor Mum must be feeling Dad's absence more than I realised.

23

My life is going from bad to worse. True, Ryan rang me and doesn't seem to mind about the horse riding with Jowan, but Chloe's just told me when we're finally going to The Club. 'This Friday night, Essie. Erik will take us to my place after school and you can stay over afterwards. We'll get back late.'

At first, my stomach gives a lurch and releases all that fluttering that people call butterflies. But mine fold their wings and plummet to my feet. 'Friday night?' It comes out as a squeak. I'm appalled, but Chloe is business-like.

'Yes, we won't leave for The Club until ten. My parents are away that weekend so there won't be any problems.' She looks at me as she says 'problems' while I register the first ever reference to her parents.

Then it fully hits me: Friday night! That's when we're doing the last practice together with the band. Kris and Marty can't practice the next few weeks since it's their first practice exams. Straight after that, it's the talent quest. Beth was even going to come this week and stay over with *me*. The band won't understand, and I won't be able to explain it either. Chloe would never understand me throwing up a perfect opportunity that she's engineered, but more importantly, I do want to go out with Ryan. I've longed for this.

This is not a topic I can ask anyone about. Mary's in the band but I know what she'll say. Laila doesn't believe in dating so that's a no brainer. Mum would have a fit as soon as I said the first sentence. 'Oh Mum, just going to The Club Friday night. The band would be cool with that, don't you think?' Not. Even Beth's going to be upset, even though she would understand about seeing the guy you like. This is her way of seeing Marty this weekend before he hibernates to study. They've had it on ever since I first took her to the youth-club barbecue on the beach. Even Chloe's parents, who must be progressive when it comes to what their kids are allowed to do, don't seem to know about this 'excursion'. Or about Derek, I suspect. Mum would not like Derek. I'm sure she'd like Ryan though.

There's Josephine, but she's already warned me about guys. Did she mean Ryan specifically? Nanna mightn't know what The Club is, so I won't ask her. She might ring Mum to ask for an explanation. Aunty Joy can smile at my nails, but she'd be texting Mum the instant I'm out the shop if I told her of my predicament. No way around it, I'm going to have to miss the practice.

Jowan is struck dumb. The dogs and I are down on the beach and I've just told him I can't make it. He dismounts and holds the reins in his hands, switching them from one to the other. I haven't seen him do that before. I watch his hands, while I can feel him staring at me. I can't meet his eyes. Why should it matter what he thinks anyway?

'If you must know—' did he ask? '—I have the chance to go out.'

'Go out?' From Jowan's mouth those words don't sound significant enough. I glance up to see how he's taking it. His expression is incredulous. 'Essie? This is the last real practice together. We need you.' There's silence, from me, that is. Behind us, the sea is swelling, crashing around our feet. A seagull cries. Jowan keeps trying. 'I thought you liked the band.'

That brings my head up again. 'I do. I'll be able to come to the next one. I know the guys won't be there, but you and me and Mary can still practice.'

'It won't be the same and you know it. You said yes when we decided the time last week.'

'I didn't know the date of this—excursion, then. Chloe's only just made the final arrangements.'

'Chloe?' Jowan says it quickly and he takes a step closer. 'Chloe? What's she organising? How can you girls go out on a Friday night by yourselves?' He sounds like Dad and it goads me to tell more.

'Not just us. Chloe's not stupid—guys are going too.'

Jowan relaxes slightly. I wonder why. Wouldn't he be wary of guys going too?

'Guys from our class?'

'Guys that can drive us, Jowan. Chloe's boyfriend, Ashleigh's, and her brother.' Why is he so bothered about it? Because he's from up north, I guess. Bet he's heard bad press about towns at night. 'It'll be okay,' I carry on. 'I've been looking forward to it, that's all.' He should understand that. I glance up to see how he's going and I see the flash of knowledge in his eyes that changes to concern and something else I can't read.

'Ryan Kitto?' is all he says. I don't like his tone. How does he know who Ashleigh's brother is anyway? My face feels like stone. This is none of Jowan's business.

He senses I've said enough. 'Okay,' he says with a sigh. Then, 'Shall we ride?'

All of a sudden, I'm panicking, I can't get caught again. Though *I wish I could.* I don't realise I've said the last bit aloud.

'Well, let's go then.' He hands out the second helmet.

'But I can't today, I'm sorry.' I start babbling. 'I have to get back and finish my maths homework. I'm behind, and if I'm to go out Friday night ...' Did I actually say that? I, who have never been overly concerned with homework?

Jowan's eyes narrow. Now would be the time he could tell me what a bitch I am, but he doesn't. He shrugs. 'Suit yourself.' He swings up onto Elaine, no saddle again. It's when he's about to move off that he tells me what he thinks. He doesn't even sound angry, just sad, and I think that's worse. I'd know what to do with his anger: reject it or throw it back, but his quiet words seep in where I don't want them.

'Essie, you're barking up the wrong tree—don't you know? Just be yourself. Don't clip your wings, let go and fly with real friends, not like this. Sometimes you can't fly on your own.'

Fly? That stupid riddle of his. Is that all he can think of? And I am going with friends, I won't be on my own. What on earth does he mean? I watch him as he canters up the beach. Elaine's mane and tail make her look as if *she's* flying. I blow out a breath. It must be so simple to be a horse.

24

It's Friday night and I'm at Chloe's at last. Her bedroom looks like a model agency before a photoshoot. Not that I've seen one, but I can imagine it: clothes scattered everywhere and makeup covering the dressing table. I feel like a music star getting ready for my first public appearance. Tonight could begin my deep and beautiful relationship with Ryan. Maybe in a year or so we'll be together all the time and we'll never want to be apart.

Getting here has been tricky. Mum didn't want me to stay over, but I'm fifteen, she can't very well stop me without acting like a tyrant. When I say there won't be movies, she relents slightly, but still insists on dropping me over. She tells me to always keep my phone with me and switched on.

'If you need anything, I'm at home, okay?' She says this outside Chloe's house. I stare at her before she leans over to kiss me—it's as if she knows what I'm about to do, but she couldn't, could she? I kiss her back before she gets the idea to walk me up to the front door and have a word with Chloe's mum. I can't get out of the car quick enough. Chloe would think shows of affection with parents are immature, and right now I can't afford to be seen as immature.

It takes all evening to get dressed. I have a top of my own, but Chloe says it doesn't do much for me. She has one that fits me but my bust bursts out the top of it and my belly button out the bottom. Chloe says that looks better. 'Pity your belly button isn't pierced.' Hers is, of course. I wear one of her skirts too, shiny and short. At least I have my own shoes. Chloe puts a belt on me, pulling it down on my hips. I wonder if it makes them look bigger, but she says they're fine. Guess she'd know.

Chloe gets herself ready first and then fixes up my hair after I've already done it. She wants to cut one side but I say no to that. Her sculpting wax is stronger than mine and in no time all my face is framed by curls. More curls fall down my back. It doesn't look too bad in the mirror, but I don't recognise myself.

When I say so, Chloe says, 'You want to get into The Club or not?' Guess I have to look eighteen, but Josephine must be over eighteen and she doesn't look like this. Chloe says she and Ashleigh have done this before so she knows what works on the bouncers. 'The Club's chilled,' she says. 'They just want to sell booze.'

Surely that can't be true. Imagine if Dad heard that. I firmly put Dad out of my mind.

At ten, Derek arrives. 'Ashleigh and Ryan will go with Brett and meet us there,' Chloe informs me. Has Ashleigh told Brett she's eighteen or what? When Derek walks in his eyes widen at me. 'Hot ace. Whadya know, the ugly duckling turns.' There's a look on his face that's off-putting. *Ugly duckling?* He doesn't say it in the same tone Jowan said 'swan'. Chloe pulls Derek out through the front door and I grab my tiny handbag and throw it over my shoulder. The door clicks behind us.

I sit in the back rubbing the sparkly nail polish Chloe's put on. She's shared all her stuff with me, and I haven't thanked her properly. I lean forward but hesitate. Chloe and Derek are talking in low voices, her hand on his thigh, and I settle back in my seat to ponder whether I may be a swan yet.

There's a spot of tension as we get out of the car. The next few minutes will determine whether Chloe and I will get into The Club or not. Even Derek's not eighteen but at least tonight he looks it. Do I?

'Come on, Essie.' Chloe's snakey, but I don't strike back. 'Look happy,' she snaps. Derek cracks a joke as we wait in line. Chloe forces a laugh. I don't think it's funny, but I try and look as though I understand. There are some other kids from senior school—also not eighteen. We all ignore each other. The line gradually diminishes and it's our turn to pass over our ID. Chloe brushes her hand against the bouncer's as he looks at hers and she grins at him. I've never seen that look on Chloe's face before. The guy doesn't seem to have noticed but he waves us through.

'See, you just have to be confident,' Chloe says. 'If you hang back they get suspicious.'

Inside, it's dark. Mum would call it dingy. The band is so noisy we have to shout. And so does everyone else. There's a sweet smell I don't care for and most of the girls that I can see are wearing even less than Chloe and me. Then Ryan sees us. I watch him make his way over between the dancers. He looks pleased with me, even more than Derek. He twirls me around once and kisses me on the nose. I don't catch what he says exactly, since he whispers it in my ear, but by the look on his face it was good. He gets us a drink first, but there's nowhere to sit, so we stand in a corner, me sipping my drink. Ryan swallows his straight down. Mine looks like orange juice but there's a bitter taste to it. I'm determined to make it last.

Ryan pulls me over to dance. 'C'mon,' he shouts. I put the

glass on a window ledge and follow him into the fray. The strobes pick up the white parts of his shirt and turn them purple. He's grinning. It's the first time I've seen him so animated and I'm not sure whether to be happy or not. I'm still getting used to this whole scene. Could I get to like this noise and crush of bodies? Ryan's smiling at me but I've missed what he said again. He's so good looking, even girls dancing with partners of their own are staring at him. I return his smile and try to put the rhythm from our band's songs into practice here.

Now it's fun. Ryan's clapping, nodding at me. 'You're a hot dancer,' he shouts. Me? He dances closer and puts his hands on my hips. I'm surprised how good it feels. When the music changes to a quieter song, he draws me close and manoeuvres me around the floor. We bump into people and he steps on my shoes a lot, but I don't mind. I smile up at him and he kisses my lips. It's better than at the town park. Now I know he must feel the same as me. The song stops but I wish it would go on and on. Ryan takes me back to where we were standing before, but my glass is gone. 'I'll get you another,' he says and goes to the bar.

Another guy sidles up to me while I'm waiting and starts chatting, though I can't tell what he's saying. He seems okay, but when Ryan comes back he moves on. 'Was he bothering you?' Ryan asks. I shake my head. The drink is different this time. Coke—but it also tastes bitter. Chloe would say my palate is immature, so I try not to grimace.

'What's in it?' I ask.

'Just Bacardi,' but he's grinning at me as if he's told a joke. I take another sip.

'Like it?'

I don't but I shrug and smile. Should I be buying him a drink? Chloe didn't tell me the etiquette of club going, only how to get in. There are a lot of girls dancing in a group. The guy who spoke to me starts dancing with them. Guess this is how you meet people. Though how you get to have a decent conversation is beyond me. Ashleigh walks past me with Brett on the way to the bar. I grin at her but she doesn't even acknowledge me. I feel an instant prick of hurt until I remember Chloe saying we mustn't spend time together in case the bouncers realise we're too young.

Ryan pulls me into the dancing again. The only dancing I've ever done is the Maypole which I enjoyed, and the private stuff in my room listening to music, but I like this too. The best bits are when Ryan's arms are around me in the slower songs, or the way he snuggles his face into my neck. In a fast song, he still manages to hold my hand. I feel like I have energy to dance all night. But when we take a breather and he gets me another drink, I know this isn't really my scene. I'd rather be dancing with Ryan on the beach than here. Some guys stare at me and I feel exposed. At least I know Ryan. I see Chloe a few times but she's too taken up with Derek to notice me.

I try not to drink all the glasses Ryan brings and just have sips. I hope it's not as many as it feels. In the next dance, I trip and Ryan catches me before I fall. He thinks it's funny, but I try to say 'no more drinks'. Ryan doesn't take any notice.

Some people have left and I lose track of time. I have no idea how long we've been here and my feet are just starting to hurt, when Ryan shouts at me. 'Want to go?'

I don't know what he means or where to—Chloe's, I hope—but it can't be as noisy, and I nod at him. He goes to find Derek. I've not seen Ashleigh or Brett again. She's done a good job of keeping him away from Chloe and me. But maybe I could fool Brett tonight. I'm trying to look like I'm sipping another drink—I lost the last one too—when a guy behind me slips his arms around my middle, a bit too high and they brush my breasts.

'Hey, let go!' But he doesn't hear me. I can smell his beer-breath and I squirm to get out of his grasp. We must look like we're dancing. Is that why no one helps? I can hardly breathe from the panic. What will he do? He's strong enough to drag me outside. His face keeps coming closer and I turn mine away.

Then Ryan's there. 'Get your hands off my girl.' He says a few other words too. Derek's with him, and the guy releases me and holds his hands up.

'Should look after a chick like her, mate.'

Ryan's face is transformed. Gone is the handsome guy. His cheeks are red, the veins in his neck stick out, his mouth curls. He doesn't even open it properly to answer but I know what he's saying. 'That's what I'm doing.' I try to fight down the fear that the other guy ignited and now is fanned by Ryan's anger.

The guy is a lot older than Ryan. What could Ryan do if he picked a fight? Right here in The Club? Would Ryan's life-saving training be enough to get him through? What if we all get arrested? Fortunately, the guy thinks we're not worth the trouble and disappears into the crowd.

'Thanks,' I mouth to Ryan. I can't believe how shaky I feel, and I let him steer me outside. I so do not want to do this again. Dancing is fine but I will never come here again. Chloe has joined Derek behind us. The fresh air rushes into my lungs and I feel dizzy. 'I'm so glad you came back just then.'

'He didn't touch you, did he?' Ryan still looks like he'll go back and punch the guy.

I stare at Ryan. I didn't think he'd be like this. Josephine's words about guys come back to me. And my first moment of wariness is born. 'Only what you saw.'

Ryan's hands relax, his tension lessens. 'No harm done then, eh?'

'Guess not.' I'm not sure what he means by no harm done. A caring hug would be good right now, but it feels like he wasn't protecting me from that guy at all, just his own male ego.

Ryan seems back to normal, but I don't totally relax. What would have happened if he didn't return? The guy in The Club was strong and didn't take me seriously. That feeling of powerlessness was overwhelming, like you're caught in a rip and there's nothing you can do. You have to go with it or drown.

Ryan and I sit in the back of the car. He puts his arm around me and I move closer for the comfort, but even before the car moves out of the parking lot, he starts kissing me.

25

I should be happy. Isn't being with Ryan what I've dreamt of all term? Maybe I'm still on the back foot from that guy grabbing me in The Club. I feel like I'm in a fishbowl. Derek can see us kissing in the mirror I'm sure. I'm so embarrassed I can't shut off. Derek murmurs to Chloe, and she giggles.

At least it's not a long distance to Chloe's house. As soon as we stop, I slip from Ryan's circle and out of the car. It'll be better inside where we'll have coffee and supper. Then we can talk more. This time Brett and Ashleigh turn up. When we go in the lounge she keeps Brett occupied. There's no small talk with him allowed. Chloe and I were briefed about that too. He looks twenty-five. Surely a guy that old could work out that Ashleigh isn't old enough for The Club. Though she does look like a model tonight.

Chloe turns the coffeemaker on so people can get a cup when they feel like it. I lay the plate of carrot sticks and avocado dip—no hummus tonight due to the garlic, says Chloe—on the coffee table. I thought Tim Tams would be good and had brought some, but Chloe was shocked. 'You want Brett to work out how young we are? Besides, he'd think we weren't serious about our fitness.' It sure is the survival of the fittest in this world.

What will everyone do now? Eat supper? Talk? Go home? They don't look like the sort of people who play games. I've picked up a carrot stick and dip—I'm starving since I was too nervous to eat dinner—when Ryan asks me to go with him to another room. 'We'll be alone.' He looks into my eyes as if he's hypnotising me, and I feel self-conscious again. But then I wonder if he did know how I felt in the back seat of the car. We'll be able to kiss without anyone watching. And talk more, I hope. There's lots of stuff I want to ask him.

'Okay,' I say.

Chloe smirks at me as I get up. Derek's turned on the TV and there's a late sports show on. Ryan takes me into Erik's room. I wonder where he is. Erik has windsurfing posters on his wall. Is he a windsurfer? I don't get to think too much about it, for Ryan's pulling me down onto the bed—there are no chairs in Erik's room—and he kisses me again. Why doesn't he say something? Like: *How was your week? You're amazing, Essie,* would be nice.

It's different from the back of the car. I thought I'd feel better because no one's watching but Ryan kisses me too hard. I'm not sure if that's exciting or not, and he's pushing down. I feel his weight on me, that feels okay. But then his hand comes up my leg before I take my next breath, which is delayed because of Ryan's kissing. My shoes make two thumps on the carpet. His hand comes up again. I can't concentrate on the kissing and I try to sit up.

'Mmm,' I try to talk, but my mouth is full of Ryan. I push his chest with the one hand I find is free. 'Ryan—' But he's not listening. I hear his zip. 'No.'

I manage to kick a leg up, which only settles him down closer. All of a sudden, a scene from that horrible movie I saw flashes into my head. It's me, I'm the one being followed by a handheld camera.

'Ryan, no!' I know I've wondered what doing it might be like, but right now I'm not prepared. Surely, it's not meant to be like this. 'Ryan—' I make a final effort. I don't care what anyone thinks. I shout, 'Stop!' It's almost a scream. That breaks his focus.

I'm shaking. He rolls back, breathing hard, frowning. 'What's wrong? I thought you wanted it.'

He doesn't say anything about liking me and I have to ask. 'Don't you care for me, Ryan? Love me?' But I know the answer before I see the puzzled expression creep over his features and reach his eyes.

'Love? This is sex, Essie. Let's have some fun. You don't have to be in love.'

But I do. I want him to love me, and I know this is not right for me. Still, I ask, 'What about the note saying you cared for me?'

He frowns. 'What note?'

My heart plummets. I'm wobbly but I stand up, in case he tries again. My right foot finds one of my shoes; the other one isn't anywhere close. The puzzlement on Ryan's face has turned dark. He pulls up his jeans, zips them, snaps them shut. 'You know what you are, Essie, you're just a tease. You don't get dressed up like that, lead a guy on and renege at the last minute—'

I don't wait to hear anymore. I have to get out. The only way I know is through the lounge. My eyes are blurred as I head for the front door. One of the guys says something, Ryan answers and they laugh. I feel like Noah must have, building a boat when no one had ever seen rain. To them, I'm just a loser.

No one comes after me and it's not until I'm a street away that I realise I've left behind my coat, one shoe, and handbag with my mobile in it. And my bra is undone. How did he do that without my noticing? Guess Erik will wonder why a girl's shoe is under his bed. How mortifying. I can't possibly go back, nor can I go home yet, and I end up near the jetty. I walk to the very end where Dad and I used to hang out.

My first thought is I'll have no friends at all after this, and then I can't believe how stupid I've been. I wish I could wash my face in the seawater, but makeup needs special remover, which is in my overnight bag, also at Chloe's. Jowan was right: I am trying to be someone I'm not. Just being at The Club showed me that, and Ryan? How did I read him so wrong? I thought he liked me—that note gave me so much hope. Fancy him denying he wrote it. Then I remember Chloe's smirk when she finally squeezed it out of me that I'd found a note in my locker. *Chloe.* It's like she's been engineering my life this whole term. Toe the line, get a date with Ryan. Did Ryan ever care for me at all, or was it Chloe making it sound like he did?

I've been so blind, just living a piece of music another person has written for me. Dad said it too—I have to write my own. I've had no faith in myself at all, but I feel very rudely awoken. It's humbling, though humiliating might be a better word.

The tide is high and I dip one set of toes in the water. The sea is so calm tonight. Maybe faith in yourself is like a bucket of water: you never know what's in it until it gets bumped. And have I been bumped! *Essie, how could you have been so gullible?* I've fabricated a romance in my mind. The Ryan I thought I knew isn't even real.

In my darkest hour, I finally talk to God, which I should

141

have done before, but I'd been flying alone without him. I sit there, listening. I don't hear anything other than the gentle lapping of the water, but my shaking subsides. I feel as though a warm cloak settles around me as light as feathers, and I know I'm not alone.

Not long afterwards, Dad finds me.

26

'Dad.' The shaking starts again. I've finally noticed the cold. He takes off his coat and puts it around my shoulders. He doesn't say anything, and I burst into tears. He sits beside me and holds me. It makes me feel like I'm ten again. Safe. The sobs subside.

'How did you know I was here?'

'You weren't at Chloe's. The jetty was my best bet.'

'I've stuffed up,' I say through the sniffs. Dad leans his cheek against mine and I can feel the wetness on his. Bet he's dying to know what happened. 'You won't want to know,' I say, just in case.

'Essie, you're my daughter and I love you. It's all that matters.'

That starts the tears again. I just want to go to my room. I can't bear to talk about it with him right now.

He understands. 'Come on.' He pulls me up. 'Let's get you home.'

On the way back I think how I'd been longing to meet him on the jetty but never did I think it would be like this.

Mum's pretty shocked when Dad brings me home and she sees

what I've got on—or not got on—but she doesn't say much. Dad must have given her one of their secret signs. She's so relieved she cries as well. I have a shower, not before Mum asks me the question: did I need to go to a doctor? So I tell her some of what happened. It helps a bit. I scrub off the makeup and go straight to bed with a hot chocolate and a sedative from Mum. It's 5am.

I sleep almost to lunch time. Dad and Mum don't even ground me. I thought I would be isolated for a month at least, miss out on the talent quest, everything. As it happens, I ground myself for a while. Not for punishment. I just don't feel like meeting people yet or facing the kids at school. Everyone will know about it by Tuesday.

Dad's stayed home today and it feels good. When I see him on the couch, I sit beside him and he puts his arm around me like he used to. I flinch but try not to show it. After Friday night I don't feel like being hugged by any guy, even Dad, and I feel bad about it. He must have noticed as he takes his arm away. He even turns the footy off. We sit quietly for a while. Then I tell him what I did.

'I went to The Club and the guy I really like, he almost, almost—' But I can't get it out and Dad's whispering things to me. I can't hear them, but his voice is calming. 'I'm really sorry.'

'So am I.' Dad finds a hanky for me; my nose is running. 'I should have taken more interest.'

'Like answering my texts?'

He sighs. 'Yes.'

'I've been texting you for yonks before the emails.'

He groans. 'Oh Es, I'm so sorry. The company gave me a phone with a new number. I didn't think to say I'd cancelled my old one. My head's full of fog lately – I can't remember anything.'

I sniff. 'I should have tried harder to talk to you, but you

144

were so tired.'

He shakes his head. 'No, it's me. Work isn't worth missing out on stuff with you and Merrie.'

'She doesn't like being called that now.' He groans again. Then I add, 'Like, missing out on my piano recital and Merryn's concert?'

He chuckles finally. 'Yeah.' Then he says, 'I've stuffed up big time.' He turns to me. 'Es, we are what we worship, what we spend the most time on.'

'Like your work became your most important thing?' I think how Ryan could only talk about his sports achievements on the phone.

Dad sighs. 'I didn't want it to be, but it looks like that's what's happened. It's dangerous because it can be taken away and then I would have nothing.'

'So that's why you said what we believe in is who we are—it can't be taken away?'

'Yeah.'

Looks like we've both had a shake up and I tell him things that have been burning in me for weeks. 'We have a band now.'

'Who's in the band? Jowan?'

'Yeah, and a couple of guys from school and a girl called Mary. She's got a great voice.' Hope they'll still want me. 'You know, Dad—' I stop and take a breath. 'I really liked this guy—' I'm determined not to cry '—but he didn't like me at all, not for myself.' My voice rises on 'myself' and Dad leans a little closer. Why don't we have words on our foreheads: *Handle with care, only fifteen, in training for relationships*. I thought Ryan was kind and cared for me. What a joke.

'Maybe if I'd been around more you wouldn't have been fooled by a punk.' Dad makes me smile, even if he does sound like he wants to punch Ryan.

'It's okay, Dad. I think I learned enough last night to last me awhile—it's like waking up after a hundred years.' I must have been on another planet.

Dad truly surprises me. I thought he'd be on about all the rules I've broken but he doesn't. All that matters is that he loves me, and I tell him too. 'I love you, Dad.'

He squeezes my hand. 'I'm sorry I didn't realise you were unhappy.'

His head rests against mine. 'Your mum was worried last night.'

'Why? She knew I was at Chloe's.'

Dad grunts expressively. Point taken.

'Actually, Chloe has been bothering me too. She's my friend but I can't work her out. When I'm with her I feel I'm not, well, good enough to be her friend, like she wants me to be like her, but it's too hard.' It sounds awful coming out of my mouth. Mum would scurry around me and say I am good enough, that I'm loved by God and my family, etcetera. Dad says none of those things.

He asks me questions. 'Does she ask how you are? What you like to do? What your ideas are?'

'No.'

'Do you have to do what she wants, or she doesn't accept you?'

'She goes quiet on me, ignores me if I disagree.'

'Do you think she's trying to change you?'

I don't answer that one. Why couldn't I see that Mary's, Laila's or Beth's kindness was so different from Chloe's attitude towards me?

'Es, some people are insecure and need control over their

environment or over a person to feel right and important. It happens in the workplace too.'

It's a new thought thinking of Chloe as insecure. And I think about how I've never met her parents. How must she feel about them not being home much?

'Tell Mum what you just told me, you might be surprised by what she says.'

'Thanks, Dad.' I smile at him. 'How did you know to come last night?'

'Ah.' He pauses, then sighs. 'It was Jowan. He rang—'

'Jowan?' I draw back.

'Don't be hard on him, sweetheart. He struggled with it a lot, but he couldn't sleep. Finally, he rang your mother—he felt you were in some sort of trouble.'

Maybe he knew what Ryan would be like? Would I have listened if he'd told me? Probably not. Then I realise what he was trying to tell me by not flying alone without my friends. He knew Chloe and Ryan weren't my true friends.

27

When my gear, including one shoe, arrives on Sunday afternoon, I know I won't cope with school the next day. I imagine Erik coming out of his room at dinner time with the shoe between finger and thumb, his pinkie in the air. 'This yours, Chloe?' Then she'd explain and explain again the next day at school. Mum doesn't mind me taking a week off. She sends an email to Ms Clemo, my home teacher so I can study online at home.

Today, I've cut my nails. Not only because I was asked to, but as a celebration of who I am. Whenever I need a break from study, I practice my pieces. If I do well, I'll be able to take piano in Year 12, then maybe the Conservatory, who knows. If anyone thinks that's nerdy, it's too bad. I've realised how discriminatory I've been, not just to myself but to others as well.

When I feel up to it, I take Dad's advice and ask Mum about Chloe. She tells me a story. 'Eseld, she reminds me of a girl I knew in first year uni. She was in second year and took me under her wing. She helped me a lot at first, even gave me gifts, took me out to cafés. I looked up to her, but she wanted to change my life.

I nod.

'If I said no about anything or couldn't come with her anywhere, she threw a tantrum,' Mum says. 'One time she threw a book at me and said I wasn't a good friend. Another day she said she'd kill herself if I didn't come visit her. Sometimes I had to do dangerous things, like walk home in the dark. Mum knew there was something wrong because I had changed and always had to go out when there was study to do. But she didn't understand and I couldn't explain. There weren't words then, that we knew of, for this sort of manipulative behaviour.'

'Is there now?'

She nods. 'It's called gaslighting, named after an old classic movie. Gaslighters often have their own problems and can turn a kind, confident person into a nervous wreck in no time at all.'

Poor Mum. And I thought she wouldn't understand what I'd been going through. I hold her hand. 'So how did you get out of it?'

'I started calling her bluff. When she said she would do such and such if I didn't come or agree with her, I said, "All right, that's your choice." After a while it felt like her control over me was slipping.' So I could have told Chloe that I didn't care about a date with Ryan? Would she have believed me?

'So that's why you didn't like me spending time with Chloe?'

Mum squeezes my hand. 'I wasn't sure, but I could see she didn't have your best interests at heart or she would want to visit you at your house and do things you like to do too.' She hugged me and sat back. 'If you want to still be friends with her you'll need to set some limits. Be yourself, so you're not feeding her behaviour.'

I find it hard to breathe suddenly. I still feel that fear when I think of Chloe. There's some anger in there too, especially for the note, for manipulating me like that. 'The fallout is extreme.

She gives me the cone of silence and who knows what she's saying about me. It makes me feel like I'm in a panic.'

'It doesn't matter what people say about you. That's none of your business. Your job is to be yourself and shine, not worry about anyone else.'

'If I say I don't like the way Chloe treats me, she won't want to be friends.'

Mum nods. 'Then you let her go, and you be friends with someone else, like Beth.'

I'm quiet for a while. Mary is a great friend too, so is Laila. But they may not want to know me now.

I write some things in my journal: I don't need a boyfriend, especially not one like Ryan. I need to live without the approval of others. I guess that's what Dad meant about standing tall. It's going to be hard, but I'll put effort in with God's help. I can choose not to take notice of what Chloe thinks of me. She won't want to be my friend now anyway, but if she does, I can ask her not to talk to me the way she has been. That's a new concept for me: that I can choose how to be treated. I write that Chloe doesn't belong in my head, then I stop. Where does she belong?

My pen scratches on the paper: in my heart. That doesn't mean I have to agree with her opinions or put up with what she says, but to want what's good for her. Josephine's words come to mind: *Essie, do you want to wake up at forty and find you're still buried under what you think everybody else wants you to be?* I chew my lip as I write that it is none of my business what others want me to be. That I am me, a person who God loves and that is enough. I'll need help believing that.

I also write that it is not my fault I am fifteen and haven't had a relationship yet. What Ryan did can't be excused by my inexperience or age.

Then I list all the people I can feel normal with and be myself. Jowan is one of them. When I'm on the beach with him I can see who I am and I can relax. I'm not like him and I don't have to be. I'm me and right now that feels like a gift.

By Wednesday I feel recovered enough to take Merryn and the dogs to the beach. I know she would have told Rebecca where we're going. Mrs Tallack usually takes the kids down now while Jowan's at the stables, but I'm mentally steeling myself in case Jowan turns up. This has to be faced. I can't skulk in my room as if it is a safe tower for the rest of my life. Not now I've remembered who my real friends are. What a fool for not seeing it before. I only hope I haven't lost them.

Tyler and Vinny burst into the waves after I take their leads off. It's getting too chilly to swim without a wetsuit, but Merryn runs with them. She's found a lot more confidence, from hanging around with Rebecca I expect. I'm going to be really careful with Merryn. She's been so sweet to me the last few days, bringing me things to eat that she's made with Mum, and writing in little cards she's created like Aunty Joy does. I don't want her making mistakes like me.

Today she says, 'I'm sorry I said you'd changed. I think you're just as nice as ever.'

I stop and give her a hug. 'And I'm sorry for not looking after you better and spending time. I want you to know that you are a special person, you are you just because God loves you so don't take any notice of what others say you should do, unless it's a good thing to do of course.'

'Essie!' I turn. It's Jowan and Elaine. I still feel flat and I only give a small smile. I don't know what he thinks of me now, but I remember to tell myself that it isn't my concern. He pulls Elaine in, slips off and comes over to me. 'I heard you weren't well, I'm sorry.' He's sorry? Then I see his eyes—they're shadowed. Is he worried what I think about him dobbing on me?

I put him out of his misery. 'Thanks for ringing my mum, Friday night. Dad found me.'

'It was bad, eh?' His tone doesn't annoy me, he's sympathetic, but I don't want to talk about it with him.

'Jowan, I'm sorry about the band practice and everything.' I hope the 'everything' will include when I've hurt his feelings.

'That's cool,' he says, and he smiles. I know he's not going to make me spell it all out. He's letting me off like a real friend does. 'Come for a ride?'

'Can Merryn come too?'

'Sure, she can wear my helmet.'

I stare at him. 'You brought two?' Incredible. He's cared enough to bring two helmets after how I treated him.

He grins. 'You never know when you might need an extra one.'

Merryn squeals when I tell her. Jowan springs up first and I hand Merryn up to him. It's difficult, but Jowan takes most of her weight. He puts her in front of him and he pulls me up behind him. I still marvel at how he does that. All the digging in his mother's rockery, I guess. Tyler and Vinny watch us, grinning, front paws apart, like dragsters impatient to race. I wonder what they're thinking. Are they as happy as me?

28

Next Monday I feel like one of the dogs on hot sand as I go into school. There are a few whispers on the way to the locker room, but like Mary on that day Chloe sang scales at her, I ignore them. Or pretend to, at least. Old habits are hard to break. I see Beth first. Here comes my first apology for the day. 'Um, Beth. I'm sorry about last Friday night. Letting you down like that.'

She doesn't look as upset as I thought she would, just says, 'It's sweet. Mum took me over and, since she couldn't pick me up she finally let Marty bring me home.' She smiles happily. 'So, it worked out for the best.'

'That's good then.' I try not to sound too relieved to be let off.

Then she says, 'Are you okay, Essie?' She's heard the rumours already.

I nod. It's going to be a long day, but I'll just do my best with God's help. That's what Mum tells Merryn when she doesn't want to go to school. It still works on Merryn.

'Beth, you can come and stay over this Friday night. I'll stick to it this time.' Then I remember. 'Oh, Marty won't be at the practice though.'

Beth gives me a wink. 'I'll see what I can do.'

Fortunately, I don't see Chloe or Ashleigh before classes, but I know they're sitting behind me in maths. I don't receive any notes. None of the things I dreaded, happen, like Chloe getting up before the teacher comes in and telling the class everything about that Friday night. When I turn to go out between classes, Chloe's watching me. Her lip doesn't curl, nor does she smile. I give her a nod to show things are cool.

Mary and Laila find me at break time. They're on the way to the canteen.

They stop, and I apologise to Mary for missing the practice. She's gentle with me even though I may have ruined the band's chance of doing well in the talent quest.

'Jowan said you had a bad time. But he didn't know any details, of course,' she adds quickly, as I look up, my face hot. Then she says, 'Are you alright, really?' I know what she means. Mum asked too.

'I think so, I got out of it, before, before—' I can't stop the sudden trembling and here I thought I was ready to come back to school. I take a deep breath and let it out slowly.

Mary puts an arm round me. 'That Ryan—in some countries, he'd be flogged.'

'It was a misunderstanding,' I say. 'He thought I wanted to because I went out with him—'

'It's no excuse—it would have been date rape, and I'm sure you feel just as bad as if you were.' I'm surprised by Mary's force of feeling. It sounds as if she knows exactly what I feel like. I check out Laila but she's just looking concerned for me. Guess she wouldn't have got into my position, but her manner isn't superior. I appreciate that. And instantly, I relax.

These girls, and Beth—they mightn't see things the way I

do, but they accept me for who I am, not because of what I've done or how I look. It brings tears and I say, 'Thanks, you guys. You're great, you know that?'

'Friends matter,' Mary says.

'Yeah, I know,' and I wipe the back of my hand across my eyes. That's what I thought about Chloe and Ashleigh too, but were they really my friends? When did Chloe ever look at me the way Mary just has and ask how I truly was?

It's Laila who puts it into words. 'When we came from Iran it was friends who got us started. We were so depressed, but they helped us through.' Both Mary and I stare at her. I've never heard her speak of her previous life. Looks like Mary hasn't either. Laila doesn't say any more and we carry on to the canteen.

Mary orders a Ned Kelly pie, so do I. Laila gets a cheeseburger without the meat. 'Do you have wholemeal bread?' I ask the woman behind the counter. She shakes her head. 'Do you think you could order some, please? Many of us know white bread isn't good for our health.' Pies and pasties aren't either, but surely one every now and then won't hurt.

'You'll need to put that in writing,' the woman says, 'and I'll bring it up at our next meeting.' She smiles as though she agrees with me.

'Listen to you,' Mary says, as we head for the oval.

I laugh. 'What's the point of complaining if we're not going to do something about it?'

Near the end of lunch, we walk to the locker room. Chloe and Ashleigh are getting their books for afternoon classes. There's no avoiding them. Ashleigh turns and sees me. She seems to be deciding what to say. I've never seen that uncertain look on her face before. 'Essie—um.' Then she pulls herself together and gets on with it. 'Ryan wants to see you. There's something he needs to say. Can you come to Chloe's house Sunday morning?' Chloe's beside her, standing with an armful of books, her lips pursed.

I'm astounded. Mary raises an eyebrow, but Laila's frowning. Bet they're wondering why he doesn't do his own laundry. Ashleigh has hardly ever mentioned Ryan to me, and now this. But it's too soon. I toy with the idea of saying I'm grounded but I have to stand on my own two feet.

'Can't do that, sorry,' and I add, 'I'll be going to church with my family.' I hope I've said it nicely without letting on I don't want to see Ryan right now, but maybe it shows. Chloe tightens her lips but Ashleigh definitely looks worried. They don't tease me about The Club or going to church. I'd always thought church would be on Chloe's list of 'stupid and immature'. I've just laid my life out on the road for them to trample on, but they stay on the footpath. For now.

'Maybe another time?' Ashleigh murmurs.

I give a nod, the sort that says maybe, maybe not. Then we all go into class together. From a distance, we would all have looked like friends.

29

Jowan's teaching me to ride! He says there's a horse in the stables that isn't being exercised as the owner has an illness and can't ride at the moment. A guy at the stables teaches riding too, but Jowan says I just need a few lessons and he'll help with the rest. 'I never had lessons,' he says.

Dad's not too sure about it but he's pleased I'm excited about life again. He takes Jowan and me to the stables to check everything out. I think he wants to see what the horse is like, not a huge stallion, for example.

It turns out to be a bay gelding called Wild Oscar. Good thing we saw the horse before we heard his name. There's nothing wild about Oscar. As soon as I see his soft brown eyes and touch his velvety nose, I'm in love. He snuffles my head like he knows it. I can't believe this is happening—we could never afford a horse, or to stable it, but the owner will pay for everything as long as Oscar gets ridden.

Wild Oscar comes with a saddle and I get to learn how to put it on and take it off. I'm shown how to brush him properly. There's so much to learn, but it's fun with Jowan doing the same things for Elaine. Merryn comes too. 'You must be strong,' Les, the stable hand, says to me. 'Wild Oscar's owner is a young man and Oscar will be used to a firm hand.'

I see what he means when I have my first lesson and Oscar does not want to trot around a circle. Guess he thinks he's grown out of that.

'Get him going,' Les says, who's showing me the ropes, or should I say, reins.

'Kick him in the side. You're the boss. It's for his own good.'

Oscar is already trained, so it doesn't take him long to do what's he's told as long as I know exactly what *I* want, and have the confidence to communicate it. When I tell Dad about it, he says it sounds like bringing up Merryn and me. He's joking, though when I think about it, it's probably similar to navigating friendships.

The first time Jowan and I ride along the beach with Oscar, I only fall off once. At least it's on sand and not the rocks. Oscar takes the lead from Elaine a lot. I'm certainly not proficient enough to take him out by myself. Once I'm back on Oscar, we head north up the beach. Oscar skips through the tidal pools and wets my feet. I can tell he loves the sand and water. Where the beach is more deserted, we canter. When we turn around the point there are no more houses and we gallop side by side, spray flying up between us like angels' wings. Jowan's laughing, watching me. 'Race me.'

Dad would have a fit but I knock my knees into Oscar's side and it's as if he's saying, 'Took your time'. He surges forward.

'Hey.' Jowan scrunches down in his saddle, urging Elaine to go faster.

Oscar and I are in the lead for a while – it's so exhilarating I'm almost crying. Then Elaine gains on us. I don't want to fall off at this speed and I pull on Oscar's reins. He's disappointed and shakes his head. Then we walk the horses to a sheltered cove.

We dismount and let the horses rest while Jowan and I sit and stare out at the ocean. 'That was so much fun,' I say.

He grins. 'Yeah. It's fun enjoying each ordinary moment.'

I don't think it's so ordinary but I get what he means. It's good not to be obsessing anymore, to just enjoy. It's like I'm ten again, except I know more.

It's fun just staring at the water and not having to say a thing. Finally Jowan says, 'Better get Oscar back to the stable on time.'

We canter back. The clouds look like spray off the rocks and they change from grey to pink to yellow.

'The sky here is as beautiful as back home,' Jowan says after we slow to a walk. 'Except we get more purple.'

'And here the sun dives into the ocean.'

'Yeah, it's a good place to be.'

When Beth comes over on Friday afternoon, Mum takes us to the stables. Beth rides behind Jowan while Merryn comes with me on Oscar. I get a bit of a twinge when I see Beth on Elaine behind Jowan. It was so much fun riding together like that. Poor Beth though. Did I look that bad when I fell off Elaine the first time? She can hardly stand up straight.

'Ow,' she says. 'That was amazing, but you sure pay for it.'

Jowan laughs, but I don't, for Beth's sake.

It's our last band practice tonight, so after we stable the horses, Beth and I go home for dinner. She's interested in seeing the ideas for what the band will wear in the talent quest. 'Because it's a mix of Blues, Jazz and Celtic we're going for an older style,' I say.

'How will you wear your hair?' And we discuss hairstyles. It's not stressful like talking with Chloe and Ashleigh. I can say if I don't like a style without Beth insisting I agree. She doesn't go quiet or say she's right. It's so relaxing being free to say what I truly think.

Then Beth says something random. 'You know, when we're kind to someone our brains release hormones which boost positive emotions. Radical kindness or niceness makes you live longer and age slower.' That must be why Mum looks younger than she is. I stare at Beth while I remember Chloe saying kind people were liars and Beth smiles shyly. 'I've wanted to say that to you for a while—I know you haven't had an easy time with Chloe, but my mum is a counsellor and maybe if you want any help I can pass on some tips.'

I don't say anything, just give her a hug.

Jowan's dad picks us up to take us to The Café. He says he'll be glad when we can all drive. Reckons he lives in the car lately, but he doesn't sound too annoyed.

Beth has a secret smile in place as we go in and I find out why. Marty and Kris are there. 'Thought we could give up a coupla hours of our precious study time, hey?' Marty puts his arm round Beth and she winks at me.

Marty's a nice guy, not like Ryan at all, but I think if any guy hugged me at the moment, even Jowan, I'd freeze. Even Dad's being careful. Mum reckons that feeling will pass.

When she said that the other night I asked her, 'Is that why you once said to wait until marriage before having sex? So I wouldn't have a rotten experience?' She hesitated. 'No, it's because of what your father and I believe.' Mum took a deep breath. 'Eseld, sex is wonderful and worth keeping for that special person in your life. We believe the amount of physical contact should match the amount of commitment to each other. We decided that the amount of commitment for sex equalled marriage. But if you don't agree with us, we won't turn you out or kill you.' She laughed, then stopped. We both know girls can be killed to uphold their family's honour. 'We just hope that if you choose a different path, you'll wait until you're at least eighteen before you act on it.'

Marty and Kris are not in their best form tonight. Kris apologises. 'It's the pressure.' He means their exams, not the talent quest. We know the talent quest is for fun and it doesn't matter if we don't get a place. By the time kids start coming into The Café for youth group we've relaxed more and the music flows. Mary is incredible even though she has a runny nose. She has a box of tissues too. Jowan suggests an antihistamine. Guess his family would know a lot about what stops running noses, though I've never heard him sneeze on the beach, only at school. We all hope Mary's okay, for although the guys are clever musicians, and Jowan's sax playing transports you to another world, and my keyboard fills the gaps, it's Mary who is the wild card.

We stop practising when The Café fills up and Oliver walks in with Josephine. Josephine is shining as she holds Oliver's hand. Mary digs me in the ribs and I grin. That's so cool. I'm happy for Josephine since Oliver is a truly nice guy even though he must be twenty-five. I say so to Mary and it reminds her. 'Talk about twenty-five-year-old blokes. That gym trainer Ashleigh Kitto was going out with? He's finally found out how young she is. He might lose his job and her parents are threatening to involve the police.'

'It wasn't his fault, was it?'

'Ashleigh's stepfather thinks it is.'

At the very least he must have known she wasn't eighteen to get her into The Club, unless Derek did her a fake ID too. No wonder Ashleigh and Chloe were different at school on Monday. Maybe Brett started to have suspicions on that Friday night when I ran out on Ryan. That wouldn't be what eighteen-year-olds do surely? When I'm eighteen I hope I'll know how to read a guy. I'm already learning.

Kris comes over and shows us the poster the talent quest organisers have put in shop windows and on light poles.

'It's even in the paper,' Marty adds. I see us there: *Travelling Spirits*. That was Jowan's idea and the others liked it. There are our names with the instruments we play beside them, just like on a CD cover.

'*Travelling Spirits*,' Beth says. She looks doubtful, but I know why he chose it; it's from that riddle. The one I haven't worked out yet, but he won't help me:

My garments sound loudly and
melodiously, sing clearly when
I am not resting on water or land,
a travelling spirit.

Jowan's undoing the strap on his sax when he hears Beth. 'Yeah, modern-day bards.' He grins at her. 'Telling the stories of who we are, our travel through this world. Isn't that what music is?' Like I've said, Jowan can be quite surprising.

Beth's helping me work out what she calls my boundaries for being friends with Chloe. When we get home, I tell her everything Mum said. Beth sighed. 'I'm sorry you had to go through that. You may need to not do things with them for a while. Until everything calms down.' She gives me a hug. 'Next term could be a new start.'

That makes a lot of sense. I feel freer knowing it's not up to me to work it all out and Jowan's words come back to me: *Sometimes you can't fly on your own.* He was right.

30

My jitters won't be quiet. We're in the Tavern on Jetty Road. People are milling around getting drinks, choosing tables. Will they be this noisy when the competition starts? I wonder if *Australia's Got Talent* contestants feel like this. Worse, probably, since they have to play to millions. We've set up our equipment already. Kris and Marty have walked all over the stage with leads and power boards. There's another band too, so Kris has put red electric tape on all our leads. One of the items is a senior school voice group, forty of them. Imagine all the parents and grandparents connected to that lot. Mum and Dad have brought Merryn and my grandparents. So glad Dad is here—he seems to be loosening up a lot. Nanna will have her iPhone ready to take pics. Even Aunty Joy didn't want to miss out.

I look out at the crowd filling up the Tavern to see if I can see my family. Suddenly, my heart slides down to my stomach. It couldn't be. What can I do? Ryan's out there. I check, just to be sure—polo necked shirt, cargo pants, wavy blond hair—yep, it's him. Odd, he doesn't seem so good-looking anymore. Note to self: next time, check out the guy's character better, not just his looks. I drop down beside Kris and Marty's guitars. Jowan finds me there.

'Essie? You going to sit with us down the front? It'll start soon.'

We have to sit through eight items, the voice group is on after us. 'I don't think I can do this.'

He hunkers next to me. 'We'll be fine. Mary's a bit croaky but she'll still be great. So will you, Essie, you never miss a beat.' He grins at his joke, but I can't.

'Jowan, how could Ryan know I'm in the quest?' Maybe it's nothing to do with me at all. Perhaps he has a friend who's competing.

Jowan is quiet a moment. 'Essie, the posters? Half the school's out there.'

I look up, horrified. 'Half the school?'

He realises his mistake. 'Not quite.' He leans closer, his voice is low. 'You're not flying alone, Essie. We're all with you—in formation. You can do this.' At least I'm not singing, my throat would slam shut. How do singers cope in times of stress?

'Take deep breaths. It will get better. Remember how you get Oscar to go a particular way? Your hand's firm so he'll ignore what's on either side of him. Do that Essie, ignore Ryan.' He stands up. It's as though he's holding out a hand so I can climb up on Elaine.

The deep breathing is helping. I feel calmer and take my cue to follow Jowan to the seats reserved for participants. Mary smells like eucalyptus drops, but she's smiling. 'I've dreamt of this, Essie, and because of you, it's happening.'

Amazed, I stare at her. 'Me?'

'You thought to ask me to sing in the band. Who would have known I liked singing? Only you knew.'

That lifts my spirits. 'Thanks, Mary.' Then I say, 'Ryan's here.'

She knows exactly how I feel. 'Don't take any notice of him, Essie. He's not worth the stress.'

'Yeah.' But it's hard to do. I concentrate on the other acts, praying I won't be distracted when it's our turn. All the contestants are from high schools from far afield, even from the mid-north. One girl plays the flute so well, she makes it sound like two. Another girl sings, with her mother playing the Tavern keyboard. She's not as good as Mary and I relax a bit more. The other band plays rock but we can't hear the lyrics, the bass guitar is so loud.

Then it's our turn. We're introduced: 'Travelling Spirits!', the loudspeaker says. We take our places. Mary and I have retro dresses on, the guys have 1930's hats and jackets. I give the intro. Kris comes in with the bass, then Marty's clever finger work on guitar, then Jowan's sax, mournful and beautiful. He's got incredible control.

And then Mary sings. *You fly on the wings of the wind ...* From that moment the audience is captivated; no one would know she has a cold. We've converted the song to a Blues rhythm. Each of the instruments has a few minutes of solo time like in jazz bands, and then Mary sings again. She holds the audience in her hand and when she reaches the climax everyone cheers. It's like they're travelling with her. *The ocean's waves join in with joy, You will fly with me, fly.*

Even before her last note fades, people stand for Mary as they did at the music school soirée. But here they won't sit down. When the guy at the microphone can't make himself heard, he has to shout. 'They're not just travelling spirits, folks, they're flying spirits. I hope they take us where they're going.' He makes a whoop like a disk jockey. I can't remember what else is said, nor can I remember what the voice group sing, except they are good. They must be, for when the place getters are announced, they receive third prize. The flautist gets second, and yes! We win.

The audience stands again, and we have to play the song while everyone claps and sings with us. We win $5000, but it's for equipment to set up the band and for promotion, so we can get gigs. The guys are stoked. We're given a certificate from the local mayor, who makes a speech about local talent and how wonderful it is to see young people being creative and enriching the community.

As people leave the Tavern our band huddles together before packing up. Mary says, 'I can't believe it,' and we all smile at her because we know that without her we wouldn't have won.

'Let's keep playing then, shall we?' Jowan says. Without him, there wouldn't have been a band in the first place. Marty and Kris agree.

'We'll start again after the exams,' Kris says.

We all hi-five each other and Mary gives me a squeeze. 'Thank you again for asking me. It's been so much fun.'

Everything's getting fuzzy by the time we start packing up. Mum and Dad and Merryn are waiting out the front for me while I zip up my piano and collect my music. When I turn, Ryan's there. Right in front of me. I don't say a thing—my mind is a black hole.

'Essie?' He looks uncertain, not like him at all. 'Essie, I had no idea how talented you are. You were great. If I'd known, you could have played at the Life Saving Club.'

'Thanks.' It's automatic, but I'm glad I'm not struck completely dumb. What I am struck by is how he can still move me. After all that happened? What's wrong with me? Is it his presence? I look at the floor but there's no help there.

'Essie,' he comes closer, but this I can't do. I look behind me. There's just the stage. No way out. 'Essie, I'm really sorry—I had no idea. I didn't—I mean, let me make it up to you. Could we start again? I haven't been able to get you out of my mind.'

I glance up at him. He seems to mean it. There are shadows under his eyes and he's actually holding eye contact. Is that worry or distress? Isn't this what I wanted? To hear Ryan Kitto say something meaningful? I look at the music in my hand. How will I say it? *Can* I say it? I know now there's more for me than a date with Ryan Kitto. I was searching for romance but I'm already part of a much bigger one. 'I'm sorry, Ryan. I don't want to go out—not with anyone at the moment.' I say it as firmly as I can.

He still looks distressed, but he doesn't try to change my mind. Good thing I wasn't counting on that. 'No hard feelings?'

No hard feelings. Incredible. What he did is a crime. Is he worried I'll press charges, is that it? And if I hold this against him and don't forgive him, who will it hurt in the end? Only me. I'd always be the victim. I shake my head slightly. It's too soon to say the words but I'm working on it. When I look up again, he's gone.

Everything's packed. Jowan comes over. 'Was that okay with Ryan?'

I nod. I'm glad he let me handle it myself.

Then I smile at him. 'Thanks,' I say. 'You're the greatest friend.'

On the way out to the car with my piano, I see Mrs Mangledorf. She was in the concert audience, and now she's noticed my nails. Short. But she doesn't comment. What self-control she has. This is what she does say: 'Eseld, I see you have even more talent than

I first thought. If you appreciate different styles of music, that is good. But why do you not finish the classical exams, learn all you can and then you can matriculate with music, and diversify when you reach university, no?'

It makes good sense. Good thing I'd already decided. Sounds like Mum telling me about belief systems: get a good foundation, then make up your mind. But music, like my beliefs, isn't something I'll make up my mind about later, it's already happened to me, has me in its grip now.

I smile sweetly at Mrs M. 'Okay,' is all I say. I've taken her by surprise. She was ready to fight for my musical foundation.

'You should still play in the band of course, as an extra-curricular activity.' She draws in a satisfied breath. 'I look forward to our next lesson, Eseld.'

31

We're down the beach celebrating. That's what Mum says we're doing, except she doesn't say what for. End of term? Winning the talent quest? The Tallacks have joined in. Rebecca has her whistle and plays while her family sings old Cornish folksongs. Luke turns a bucket upside down and bangs on it with a spade. The way he plays it sounds almost like a bodhran. The Tallacks are seriously talented. Some tourists visiting 'Australia's little Cornwall' stop to listen and take photos with their phones. The kids have made a huge castle. 'Like King Mark's,' Merryn says. I guess it would make a good shot for social media.

Dad and Mr Tallack cook the barbecue while the rest of us swim. It's wetsuit weather but the kids and dogs don't seem to notice. I jump in too and Jowan throws me a ball. We're playing water soccer now and it turns out to be fun, even when Jowan half drowns me trying to get the ball off me.

There's a call for lunch and we dry off before enjoying homemade burgers and locally made sausages. Merryn produces the chocolate cake she and I made last night. She's getting really good at cooking and everybody says so. It feels like Christmas and I'm dying to know what we're celebrating.

After cake, Dad stands up and says, 'I have an announcement.' I can tell by Mum's face that she knows. 'The company I work for have finally realised that I'm doing the work of two people and they've opened another office here in town for me to manage, and they'll employ someone else to manage their other office.'

'Wow,' I say. 'Does that mean you'll be home for dinner, free on Saturdays and not working on your laptop every evening?' Do I sound bitter?

Mum laughs and Dad tries to look repentant. 'I certainly expect so. There may be a little homework but not like before.'

I throw my arms around him and squeal like Rebecca. So does Merryn. It's the noisiest group hug we've ever had. He kisses the top of my head and it feels so good to be held by Dad again.

Dad's blinking as he says, 'I'll clean up after but right now I want to take my girls for ice-creams on the jetty.'

Merryn gives a whoop and I hug Dad again.

'Can we come too?' That's Rebecca. She's asking Merryn and me. Maybe she knows how special this is for us. I raise my eyebrows at Merryn and she grins.

'Sure,' I say.

Jowan rounds up his mob and we walk along the beach to the ice-cream shop—actually, the kids run and skip and Tad rides on Jowan's shoulders.

Our ice-creams are half-eaten by the time we walk down the jetty. How I longed for this just with Dad, and yet it feels good to share this moment. A moment not tarnished by Ryan's assault. Dad, Merryn and I lead the way to our special place at the end and we all sit in a group facing the sea. Merryn and I sit on either side of Dad; Rebecca plops down by Merryn and they do a fancy high-five. Jowan sits by me with Tad in his lap. We all stare at the waves as they bounce against the jetty pylons. Even

Desi is quiet as we finish our ice-creams.

Seagulls hang over us and when no one feeds them they fly off like jet fighters in formation. Then what do you know? A dolphin jumps only fifty metres out, and another. The kids 'ooh' and 'aah' like it's a fireworks display, but it's still exciting for me. I'm thinking how perfect this is and I know it's because I've finally worked out how to enjoy what Jowan calls 'the ordinary' and to just be me.

Everyone has packed up and gone and it's close to sunset. I'm here on the beach alone with the dogs. I love the way they dance. Guess it's more like bouncing and chasing and dive-bombing, but it makes me want to do it too. I roll up my jeans and join in. I dance with them. Vinny jumps around me, Tyler gives a happy yelp. I run and dance through the pattern of their crisscrossing. Spray splashes around me but I don't mind. I finally feel like a swan, transforming, skimming the water with grace, flying, rising like a travelling spirit. I hold my arms out like wings as I twirl. It reminds me of Jowan on the jetty that day protesting that I was the swan. And with the sudden realisation of a mystery unveiled, I laugh aloud, because at last I know the answer to Jowan's riddle.

The Riddle

My raiment is silent as I tread the earth
or inhabit the dwelling or disturb the water.
Sometimes my trappings and this high air
raise me over the heroes' hall,
and then the strength of the clouds
bears me widely over the people.
My garments sound loudly and
melodiously, sing clearly when
I am not resting on water or land,
a travelling spirit.

Riddle 7 from *The Book of Exeter*, c.960-980

The answer is: A swan.

Note from Author

If you find yourself in a difficult or confusing friendship, do talk about it with someone. If you are feeling depressed or you are worried about a friend, try ringing Lifeline on 13 11 14 or chat online at https://www.lifeline.org.au/

Acknowledgements

Firstly, I acknowledge the Ngadjuri, the original owners of the land where I live and where this book was written. I also acknowledge the Narungga people on whose land this book is set.

I acknowledge and thank St Aidan's Anglican Girls' School, Corinda, for the words: 'Sometimes you can't fly on your own.'

I acknowledge the use of some words from *The Book of Exeter*, a 10th century volume of Anglo-Saxon poetry, the largest and oldest known collection of Old English poetry still in existence. The riddle-poems can be found online or in the book, *The Exeter Book Riddles* translated by Keven Crossley-Holland.

Thank you to Abba for helping me always, to Rochelle Stephens for believing in this story and publishing it; to my readers, thank you for your great suggestions: Amelia Penner, Astrid Cooper, Dearne Prior, Helen, Lamb, Katie Hawke, Makayla Penner. For support, thank you to all my fellow Ekidnas; Janeen and Phil, and my local writing group, Nancy, George and Wendy for helping me with the right word and editing queries. Finally, without the creative team at Rhiza Edge *Flying Blind* wouldn't have flown off at all. I'm so thankful to you all.

About the Author

Rosanne Hawke is an Australian author of over thirty books, among them *Zenna Dare* and the *Beyond Borders* series. Rosanne was a teacher, an aid worker in Pakistan and the United Arab Emirates for ten years, and has taught Creative Writing at Tabor Adelaide. She writes of belonging and identity, cultures and faith and is the 2015 recipient of the Nance Donkin Award for a woman author who writes for children. She is a fourth-generation Cornish descendant, a bard of Cornwall, and lives in rural South Australia in an old Cornish farmhouse with underground rooms. www.rosannehawke.com